Will   Irma   Taranee   Cornelia   Hay Lin

The Light of Meridian

Adapted by JULIE KOMORN

HarperCollins *Children's Books*

This book was first published in the USA in 2004 by Volo/Hyperion Books for Children
First published in Great Britain in 2005 by HarperCollins *Children's Books*, a division of
HarperCollins Publishers Ltd.

© 2005 Disney Enterprises, Inc.

ISBN 0-00-720942-8

1 3 5 7 9 10 8 6 4 2

All Rights Reserved. No part of this book may be reproduced of transmitted in any form or by any
means, electronic or mechanical, including photocopying, recording, or by any information storage
or retrieval system, without written permission from the publisher. For information contact
HarperCollins Publishers, 77-85 Fulham Palace Road, Hammersmith, London W6 8JB.

The HarperCollins website is:
www.harpercollinschildrensbooks.co.uk

Visit www.clubwitch.co.uk

Printed and bound in Great Britain by Clays Ltd. St Ives plc.

HOW DID I GET SO DIRTY? I HOPE THAT MATT DOESN'T NOTICE!

NO, NOT AT ALL!

AM I LATE?

LUCKILY, YOU'RE EARLY! I HAVE A FAVOUR TO ASK YOU.

TODAY MY NEPHEW HAS TO REHEARSE WITH HIS GROUP. . . .

WE'RE OFF TO A GOOD START!

. . . AND I MUST TAKE CARE OF A **SPECIAL PATIENT** AT HOME. ARE YOU OKAY STAYING HERE ALONE?

NO PROBLEM!

– IN SPITE OF THE FACT THAT YOU HAVE WARNED ME OF THE CATASTROPHES THAT MIGHT HAPPEN!

HEH! HEH! SEE YOU LATER, THEN!

!!!

YOU HAVE BEEN VERY KIND! GOOD-BYE!

I DON'T BELIEVE IT!

I look forward to embracing my puppy. Kisses xxx Jackie

IT IS NOT POSSIBLE!!!

PLEASE GIVE IT TO MATT. I TRUST THAT YOU CAN DO THAT, RIGHT?

ONE

Will was fuming. And even though the cold, winter air numbed her face as she rushed out of Mr. Olsen's pet shop, it didn't numb her anger. How could this day possibly get any worse?

The day had started with great promise. All day long Will had been looking forward to going to Mr. Olsen's pet shop after school. Being Mr. Olsen's assistant was the perfect job for Will. She loved animals (especially frogs – she had a whole collection of frog toys at home). And Mr. Olsen was the sweetest, kindest man, and knew everything about taking care of all kinds of pets. He also happened to be Matt Olsen's grandfather. And Matt Olsen happened to be Will's secret crush.

Matt was sweet, adorable, and one hundred

percent dreamy. He was a year older than Will and played in a band called Cobalt Blue. Hands down, he was the biggest hunk in school. With his brown hair, tall, lanky body, and fuzzy goatee, he fit the role of lead singer and hunk perfectly. Matt loved animals, too, which just added to his charm. Those same hands that strummed a guitar could also make a cat purr lovingly or a dog cover Matt's face in licky kisses.

As Will jumped onto her bicycle outside the pet shop, she thought about the time when she had first moved to Heatherfield. She had met a lot of people those first few weeks. There were so many changes – and transformations! A new apartment, a new school, and four amazing new friends.

Whenever Will thought about how she and her friends had met, she smiled. Was it luck or magic that had brought them all together? Whatever it was, they were a rather unlikely group. Taranee was shy and inquisitive. Cornelia was headstrong but very loyal. Irma was opinionated and hysterically funny. Then there was Hay Lin, the artistic and calm one.

Despite all of their different personalities,

the friends had one major thing in common. They were a team charged with the challenge of keeping the world safe from all kinds of evil. Being empowered with magical abilities allowed them to control the elements: earth, air, fire, and water. Will had been given control of an extra-special power – the Heart of Candracar. That was the link that made their powers unite and also made Will the unsuspected (and usually reluctant) leader of the team.

An all-knowing spirit who lived in an ethereal world called Candracar had anointed Hay Lin, Cornelia, Irma, Taranee, and Will as the Guardians of the Veil. The Veil was an invisible divider between earth and the dark world of Metamoor.

It was the Guardians' job to make sure that no evil creatures crossed the twelve portals found within the Veil. According to Hay Lin's grandmother, who had once been a Guardian herself, the recent millennium had caused the Veil to grow weak. Creatures from Metamoor were able to travel through the Veil, by way of portals, which are like cosmic tunnels.

After discovering their destinies, the girls

had started to call themselves W.i.t.c.h. – an acronym of their names: Will, Irma, Taranee, Cornelia, and Hay Lin. And so far, they were doing a pretty good job of protecting earth. They had won several battles against the sinister Prince Phobos and his evil sidekick, Lord Cedric. But the girls had to be constantly aware of the dangers around them.

Today, though, even the magic Will had inside of her couldn't ease the anger she felt as she pedaled through the snowy streets of Heatherfield. Who was Jackie? What did Matt think of her? And what, Will wondered, did Matt think of Will?

Will clearly remembered the day she had first met Matt.

She was in the park trying to help save a dormouse from the school bullies, who were trying to hurt it, when he passed by. After the attack, the dormouse looked cold and hungry, and somehow Matt convinced her to take it home. It probably wasn't hard, since Will was pretty much speechless because she thought Matt was so dreamy. When he gave her his cell phone number, so that she could call him if she needed any help, Will was surprised – and touched – by his thoughtfulness. It was at that moment that her crush on Matt began.

But then Will was summoned to Candracar. She knew she couldn't take care of the wounded dormouse while she was away. So, she left the dormouse in Matt's front yard and sent him a text message asking him to take care of the little animal.

Will hoped all would be normal when she returned. Unfortunately, that was wishful thinking. She had left an astral drop – an exact replica of herself – to fill in for her while she was gone. When she got back, she was horrified to discover that her astral drop had kissed Matt! And later on had slapped him in the middle of school because of the kiss! It was a huge misunderstanding. To make matters worse, her dormouse had gotten sick from eating too many cookies. Needless to say, she still had a lot of work to do on the whole astral drop thing – and on getting back into Matt's good graces.

Taking the sick little dormouse to Matt's grandfather's pet shop was a start. She had thought it was a sign of her new, more responsible self.

When she'd brought the dormouse to the pet shop, Matt had been there. He'd introduced her to his grandfather, who'd said he was able to help the dormouse and had even offered her a job at the shop.

Matt and his grandfather were close, and sometimes Matt worked in the shop to help out. Will had figured there was always a good chance he might swing by while she was working. It had seemed like a perfect plan to get to know him better.

Until now.

Was there anyone cuter in the whole universe? Will wondered with a heavy sigh. She had thought that when she first met him. And she still did. But now it seemed as though this Jackie girl thought the same thing!

Wait a sec. Who is this boy-crazy nut I'm turning into? Will thought with a laugh.

She was not normally like that. It was usually Irma who went on and on about boys. But this crush made Will feel different – all jittery and jumpy. Even her toes tingled.

Clearly, Will's plan to help out at the store hadn't been all about animals. The possibility of seeing Matt had been an added bonus. Well, I'm off to a good start, Will thought sarcastically, feeling a bit deflated as she remembered the conversation she had had with Jackie at the shop. Matt had not stopped by. Instead, a beautiful woman had come looking for him. . . Those were two things that she hadn't expected.

Jackie, the curvy and glamorous visitor, had quickly burst Will's bubble of confidence. Right before Jackie entered the store, Will had been feeling very confident. When Mr. Olsen left to make a house call, she had felt fine staying in the shop alone. She had felt good about being left in charge of the shop – and, of course, had hoped that maybe Matt would come by at any moment. She wondered if Mr. Olsen knew that she had a megacrush on his grandson. She hoped not – that would have been mega-embarrassing!

As Will pedaled along under the chilly afternoon sun, she thought more about what had happened and got more and more upset as she replayed the scene in her head. . .

After Mr. Olsen left, a cool, snowy breeze danced into the store behind him. Will stood up straight behind the counter, her arms stretched out, fingertips resting on the counter-top. Ready and waiting for action, she hoped some clients would arrive and allow her to really show Mr. Olsen how competent she was to work in the shop.

Until then, she would have to find a way to entertain herself. She looked around. Cuddly kittens poked their heads out from a box on the floor. Rows of rubbery dog and cat toys sat next to pet shampoo bottles and comfy-looking pet beds. Cans of cat food, sacks of dog food, and a rainbow-coloured array of fish-food containers filled the shelves.

Tick Tock Tick Tock. The clock on the wall behind her kept rudely reminding her that time was moving very slowly.

Tick Tock Tick Tock. Just like school, she thought. Time had slowed to the speed of molasses.

Tick Tock Tick Tock. Maybe Matt will swing by some other time, she muttered to herself.

The gurgling fish tanks, chirping birds, and purring kittens created a soothing symphony, like a lullaby. Her eyes started to close. She was getting sleepy – very sleepy.

I'd better do my homework, she finally decided, dragging various heavy textbooks and bulky notebooks from out of her backpack and spreading them out on the counter.

She had barely opened the first book when a loud *Skreeeek!* from out in front of the shop interrupted her. Will peered through the front window just in time to see a snazzy little yellow sports car that had just pulled up.

"Hooray!" Will said out loud. "Someone's coming in!"

Dling! The bell announcing the new customer chimed throughout the store.

But this wasn't just any old customer. Into the shop strutted a tall, curvy, and sophisticated young woman. Fiery auburn hair fell dramatically around her face. A zippered, cropped, turtleneck sweater showed off her tiny waist. She wore a wraparound miniskirt low across her hips with a loose tassel belt dangling just so. A long, cream-coloured coat and leather gloves topped the ensemble off.

"Hello," the woman said in a husky voice, a gigantic, lipsticked smile on her face.

"Hello," Will replied shyly. "May I help you?"

"No, thanks," Ms. Fashion Plate said,

glancing around the store. "I'm looking for Matt." She took a confident step closer in her tall, high-heeled, black leather boots.

Even as Will replayed the girl's grand entrance in her head, a dozen questions raced through her mind. Why had she been asking for Matt? Who was she? How did she know Matt? Did he *like* her?

"Well, he's not in today," Will explained. "But if you need – "

"A piece of paper, then," the woman purred with a fake grin, her hair glistening beneath the fluorescent lights. She didn't even let Will finish her sentence .

Will walked over and ripped a piece of paper out of her notebook. "Is this okay?" she asked irritably.

"Yes, good." With a slight scowl, the young woman pulled a fancy designer pen out of her stylish, slate-coloured handbag.

Will watched her and slyly stuck out her tongue in annoyance. That made her feel a teeny-tiny bit better. But not much.

Thinking about the piece of paper in her back

pocket, Will wonderered if she really should give the note to Matt. The way Jackie had said, "Remember that I entrusted this to *you*" made Will feel like not giving the letter to Matt.

As Will carefully rode home through the snow, she wondered if it were possible that Matt had a crush on Jackie. Her mind immediately started jumping to the worst conclusions. She envisioned them on dates. Holding hands. Looking into each other's eyes. *Bleccch!* It was too much.

If only she knew what the note meant. Of course, she had already memorised what Jackie had written on the piece of paper.

I look
forward
to embracing
my puppy.
Kisses,
Jackie
XXX

"*Give it to Matt,*" Will mimicked in a deep, whispery voice, trying to do her very best Jackie imitation. "*Please remember, I entrusted this to you!*" She could still recall Jackie's tone and the way she had held the paper with two fingers.

"Grrr," Will grumbled, gripping the handlebars of her bike even tighter.

Shaking herself out of her reverie, she continued home. The snow was piling up quickly. Will rode carefully, zigzagging through the powdery mounds. Snowflakes were now falling at a sideways angle. As she pedaled she kept hearing Jackie's voice inside her head, over and over: "puppy . . . ," "kisses . . . ," "puppy . . . ," "kisses . . ."

Even though Will was bundled up in her grey fleece coat and orange woolen hat, a chill ran down her back. I have no chance against Jackie, she thought. The wind howled and blew snow into her eyes. Jackie is too sophisticated. Too beautiful. Too everything.

That did it, Will decided. "Matt won't see that piece of paper!" she said with determination as she pedaled off.

TWO

Even though it was a cold and gloomy day, Taranee sat looking out her bedroom window thinking it was the most glorious day ever. There was no sunshine, but the city was covered in a pure, white blanket of snow. There was a hush over all of Heatherfield, and the whole city seemed still. Today is perfect, she thought as she sat on her bed, hugging her knees to her chest. Yes, today was going to be the best day ever.

Taranee looked happily around her room. She knew that she was a bit of a neat freak, and her room reflected her very organised and clean ways. There was no special magic involved. Taranee was just plain neat.

Her shoes were carefully arranged on the rug alongside her bed. The computer sat on the middle of her desk without a loose paper in sight. Books, alphabetised by author's name, were evenly spaced on the shelves, right next to her CD collection. A tiny notepad, lamp, and alarm clock were set just so on her bedside table. If there was anything unusual in the room at the moment, it was the extra-bright twinkle in Taranee's eye.

She sighed and snuggled back against her pillow, feeling cosy in her long, eggplant-coloured dress. As she rested against her wicker headboard, she watched the snow accumulate outside on the windowsill. With all the various changes that had been happening to Taranee and her friends, the most recent change had been the most surprising. Being made a Guardian of the Veil, infused with magical powers, was one thing, but she never expected that the boy who she had a crush on would ever like her back!

The phone next to her bed rang, startling her and interrupting her thoughts.

"You have to tell us what's going on!" Irma's voice shrieked as soon as Taranee picked up. "We don't keep secrets from each other," she prodded.

"Yeah," added Hay Lin, who was evidently sharing Irma's phone. "I wanna know, too!"

Taranee smiled as she pictured Irma and Hay Lin huddled together on Irma's bed, both trying to listen on the same phone. She could hear the excitement in their voices – and their impatience.

"There are no secrets," Taranee reassured them, rolling her eyes behind her tiny, round specs. "I promise you, I'll fill you in on every-thing tomorrow."

"How can you be this cruel?" Irma whined. Taranee imagined Hay Lin pulling on Irma's arm, trying to get closer to the phone to hear Taranee's response.

"While you're out with your mysterious knight, we're going to be stuck in the hands of Mrs. Vargas!" Hay Lin complained. "We have an extra-credit session for biology class today." Her voice sounded a bit muffled. She was clearly not the one holding the phone. Taranee was positive that Irma was the one clutching the phone, making sure that she heard every word. Irma was pretty stubborn. Especially when she was desperate to find out a romantic scoop!

"I'm soooo sorry for you!" Taranee replied,

tossing her beaded braids over her shoulder. She was having fun teasing her friends. Their extra-credit photography workshop with Mrs. Vargas meant that Hay Lin and Irma had to go to school for a few hours. Taranee found their situation amusing. She wanted to fill her friends in on all the fantastic details, but there just wasn't time for that right now.

"Don't try to change the subject!" Irma demanded. "Tell us who he is!"

At that moment, Peter, Taranee's older brother, pushed open her bedroom door and stuck his head in. "Someone's at the front door," he announced. She could hear the notes of the doorbell ringing over his shoulder. Her stomach did a flip-flop.

Peter was a basketball hotshot and a great surfer. He faced everything with an easygoing, surfer-dude chuckle. Taranee was sure he wasn't afraid of anything.

Maybe I should ask him for some dating pointers, Taranee thought, half-jokingly. He's always so cool in social situations. What would he say if he knew that I was going out on a date?

"Sorry, girls, I have to go," Taranee blurted

out to her friends. She quickly hung up the phone before they could protest, and sat up straighter on her bed. She knew that she wasn't being exactly nice, but she had to hurry. Her date had arrived!

"Could you answer the door?" she hollered to Peter. "I'll be there in a minute!"

"Sure thing," said Peter, as cool and calm as ever.

Shoes, shoes, shoes! thought Taranee frantically as she tried to force her red ankle boots on. They weren't fitting over her thick, black winter socks. She was trying to put them on as fast as she could, but her hands were shaking!

She could hear Peter's feet pounding down the steps towards the front hall. Excitement swirled in her. She finally managed to wiggle her shoes on, and started lacing them up.

She heard Peter open the front door. "Come in," she heard him say. "Taranee will be down in a minute."

Taranee paused and leaned out her door to hear what happened next.

"Thanks," Nigel said. He sounded so polite and cute! Taranee could barely stand it. Was this really her life? Was she about to go on a date with Nigel, her secret crush? It all felt so surreal.

Hearing his voice made her swoon. She let out a nervous giggle. Nigel was at *her house*. Picking her up for *their date*! Even though she had known he was coming over, she still couldn't believe he was actually there. At her door. In her house!

She heard Peter close the front door and say, "Though I don't know how long *a minute* will take with my sister."

Taranee could just imagine the big smirk on Peter's face. She had to hurry. She didn't want to keep Nigel waiting with Peter for too long. Peter was pretty cool, but, still, he was her older brother. Who knew what he might say? Or what damage he might cause?

My coat, my coat, Taranee thought, slightly panicking. Where is it?

As Taranee hurried around her room look-ing for her coat, she thought that Nigel might be getting nervous.

I bet he is playing with his hat, like he does whenever he gets anxious, she thought.

Peter is probably being nice – at least she couldn't hear his voice, so he probably wasn't saying anything embarrassing about her! She headed downstairs – ready to face Nigel.

"Here I am!" Taranee sang out, slipping on her magenta-coloured coat, which she had just found hanging in her closet, right where it was supposed to be.

"Hello, Nigel," she said, beaming.

"Hello," Nigel replied, a wide smile spreading across his face. Nigel stood in the living room, nervously playing with his hat. *Just as I imagined,* Taranee thought with a small grin.

There he is, she thought, *standing in my house. His adorable, kind face and long, shaggy, brown hair. Oh, and that cute-boy smell, too – a pleasing mixture of fresh grass and soap.*

Their eyes locked in a sweet, private stare. Everything else in the room went blurry in Taranee's eyes.

Peter watched them, keeping as still as the plant in the front hall. He stuck his hands in his pockets, seemingly trying to blend in with the wall behind him. But it didn't matter. Neither Taranee nor Nigel were paying any attention to him.

"Well," Peter muttered, "have fun." He saw that his sister and Nigel were still in their own world. "I've got things to do," he continued, walking into the hall with exaggerated strides, his hands still crammed into the pockets of his cargo pants. "Don't try to stop me. Don't beg me," he called teasingly over his shoulder.

Again, Taranee ignored her protective and slightly goofy older brother.

"Did you pick a movie?" Taranee asked Nigel, as she grabbed her blue bag and tossed it over her shoulder.

"No, I want you to choose," Nigel said, smiling at her.

As they walked out the front door of her house, Taranee buttoned up her coat. The snow was coming down pretty hard, and she wanted to be well bundled up before heading out.

"Wait," Nigel said. He snapped open a blue umbrella and held it over Taranee's head.

Just like a gentleman in an old-fashioned, romantic movie, Taranee thought, gazing into his soft, brown eyes and focusing on keeping herself from melting.

She walked quickly down the front path. She wanted to get away from her house – and her mother – as quickly as possible. Taranee could feel her mother and brother watching from the kitchen window.

She could hear her mother's voice.

"I don't like the idea of her going out with that boy!" Taranee's mother said in an anxious tone.

"Don't worry, Mum. He's a good guy," Peter assured her.

"Maybe I was wrong to let this happen," Taranee's mother said, her voice full of worry. "Remember what he and those boys did in the museum."

"But, Mum, Nigel isn't part of Uriah's gang anymore," Peter gently reminded her. "So, relax."

Nigel had once been involved with a gang of wannabe thugs. People at school called them the Outfielders, as opposed to the Infielders, who were the popular kids. The oily-chinned, red-and-spiky-haired leader, Uriah, had had the brilliant idea of breaking into the Heatherfield Museum. The other two trouble-makers in the group, Laurent and Kurt, had liked the idea, but Nigel hadn't. He had gone along with it anyway, however, and they had all ended up getting caught. Taranee's mother just happened to be the judge at the Heatherfield courthouse – and she had sentenced them all to three months' community service at the museum.

"I just hope you're right," Taranee's mother said to Peter. In her voice, there was still a note of concern.

Taranee had no doubts about Nigel as she walked down the path with him. Nigel was as sweet and kind as she had thought from the beginning.

So far, this day was just perfect. The snow was thick and just right for making snowballs. Taranee couldn't resist. She quickly bent down, gathered some snow, and formed a nice, round ball. With perfect aim, she tossed it at Nigel, who was looking the other way.

"Gotcha!" Taranee squealed as the snow-ball made contact. *Thump.* It landed right on the side of Nigel's head.

"Ha-ha," Nigel laughed, looking down at the snow that dripped down his army-green jacket. "You know you're gonna get it now, right?" he cried, chasing after her in his thick-soled boots. He held up a big, wet snowball and aimed it in her direction.

"Well, I'll only get it if you can catch me!"

Taranee said with a giggle, as she raced ahead of Nigel.

As Taranee weaved and dodged just out of Nigel's grasp, she couldn't keep the smile off her face. Who knew that she, the shy newbie, would ever be hanging out with such a cutie! The day really is perfect, she thought, just perfect.

THREE

Cornelia had only two more maths problems to go, but her mind kept wandering. She was thinking about *him* again. The charming, blue-eyed boy who'd appeared in the swirling leaves outside her classroom window weeks ago. The one who winked at her in her daydreams.

Was it just a dream? she wondered for the gazillionth time. She felt as though she'd seen him somewhere before. But where?

She finished up the last two problems and snapped her maths book shut. Quickly stuffing her notebook and pencil into her backpack, she zipped her bag shut.

Phew! She thought. Glad I'm done with that. Homework can be such a big drag.

That morning, she had made up her

mind that she would go talk to Will. Even though Cornelia didn't truly like the idea of Will's being the leader of W.i.t.c.h., she knew she had to talk to her about her plan. The other Guardians might not like her plan, but she had to propose it.

"I finished my homework!" she shouted to her mother, who was in a different room of their posh apartment. "May I please go out now?"

"After you've cleaned up your room," her mother answered from the couch in the living room.

So, I guess that means I can go out, Cornelia said. She smiled to herself, a relieved and sneaky smirk. She looked around the pigsty she called her room, noting the papers, pens, stuffed animals, sweaters, and shoes strewn everywhere. Cornelia snapped her fingers and waited.

Then, before her eyes, her room began to transform itself magically. She stood and watched as a gentle breeze sailed through her room, swooping up her bow-tied teddy bear and her fuzzy green bunny from the floor and placing them gently on her pillow. Her desk drawer flew open to welcome the pens, pencils, and erasers that were coming in for a landing. Her sheets and comforter were neatly tucked into the bed corners; her pillows were fluffed, books returned to the shelf, and sweaters and shirts neatly folded and placed in the closet. Her boots and slippers landed in a perfect row by the door. The laces of her ice skates tied themselves together and hung themselves on their hooks on the wall.

Cornelia grinned, loving her powers. She could control the earth *and* clean up her room with a swift movement of her hand. Or course, that particular trick had taken some time to master, but now she was capable of doing her cleanup in just a few seconds. While she loved using her powers to battle Prince Phobos's minions and the evildoers from Metamoor, this cleanup trick was rather handy.

As things flew back into place, something caught her eye. Right beneath her bed, the corner of a turquoise-coloured book was sticking out. It was her old journal!

She hurried over and picked it up. Pieces of paper stuck out haphazardly. "My diary from last year," she whispered. "With all my old memories." She flipped through the pages, and the book made a fanlike *frushh* sound. "I thought I'd lost it," she sighed, feeling nostalgic about the time when she had written in the book every day. Suddenly, her eyes grew wide as she began to read the writing on the page in front of her. It was a poem surrounded by hand-drawn, pastel swirls, leaves, and flowers.

You are nice
You are lively
You are the friend I like
You are nice
You are okay
Stay the same

It was signed, in curly script, *Elyon*.

"Elyon!" Cornelia gasped when she saw the flowery signature.

Back then, things were so different, she thought, remembering the previous summer. That was before Cornelia and her friends had become magical Guardians of the Veil. Before Elyon had run off to Metamoor. Before Elyon had turned against them and joined the enemy.

Cornelia still found the situation very

painful and hard to comprehend. How could her friend Elyon have become so cruel, and such a real threat to the Guardians?

Other worlds, special powers, enemies, Elyon . . . yes, a lot had definitely changed since that poem was written, Cornelia thought with a sigh.

Leaning back against her blue-ruffled pillow, Cornelia crossed her legs and flipped through the pages of the diary. The various entries jogged so many memories. One page in particular sent her back to a specific moment. It stuck out clearly in her mind.

She closed her eyes, and the memory came flooding back to her.

Cornelia was standing in the center of an ice rink. She had just won a figure-skating competition and been awarded a shiny bronze medal for her performance. Her face was flushed, and she was wearing her shiny, bright, green-and-turquoise costume. Her long, blonde hair was pulled back, and a pretty band of flowers adorned her bun. The crowd applauded and cheered. Cornelia held up her medal, which was strung on a purple ribbon around her neck.

She remembered looking out proudly into the crowd.

Elyon was there, watching from just behind the railing of the rink. Cornelia could see the happiness Elyon felt for her friend's victory bursting out of her. "Third place," Elyon called out to her excitedly. "You were great! I knew you could do it!"

After her bow, Cornelia skated over to where her friend stood. "I still can't believe it," Cornelia beamed back at Elyon, a bit out of breath. Elyon leaned over the blue metal railing and gave her a huge hug.

"Next time, I bet you'll win the gold," she said proudly.

"I'll always be a winner as long as you're around," Cornelia said emotionally, hugging her friend back tightly. She looked at Elyon, her blue eyes growing wide and a little misty. "You are my secret lucky charm, Ellie!"

After the competition was over, Elyon went back to the locker room with Cornelia and helped gather her stuff together, while Cornelia sat on a nearby bench and unlaced her skates. Most of the other skaters had already left, and the room was quiet. Cornelia could tell that

Elyon had something on her mind as she stood packing Cornelia's warm-up clothes into the gym bag. Finally, Elyon looked up.

"Anyway, is it true?" Elyon asked, zipping the gym bag closed. She slung it across her shoulder, tossing one of her long braids behind her. "Did you really turn down a date with Pete?"

"Yes," Cornelia replied quickly as she pulled off a skate. "And you know why, Elyon." Cornelia looked down at her feet, a serious look on her face.

"Because of the boy in your dreams?" Elyon asked compassionately.

Cornelia came back to reality. The memory was fading. She sat on her bed with the diary lying open on her lap. "What happened to us – to Elyon?" she asked out loud, her voice filled with hurt and confusion. "Why have we become enemies?"

Her forehead became creased, and her eyes filled up with tears she could no longer hold back. The memory reminded her painfully of how close she and Elyon had been and how special a friendship they had once had.

How could someone who knew all her secret thoughts and dreams have turned on her so suddenly and so completely? Cornelia looked back down at the diary and continued reading the passage in it.

Every detail of that day came rushing back to her. She even remembered exactly what she had been wearing – a new, sporty, red-and-white sweat suit and white sneakers. Elyon had had on a purple-and-blue dress.

Cornelia's thoughts once again drifted back to that day. . .

After Cornelia had finished changing, the two friends left the ice skating rink together and walked home through the park. On the way, they continued the conversation about Cornelia's dream boy.

It was a dazzling, sunny afternoon, and people were sprawled out along the grassy hills surrounding the park. Everyone seemed to be out, enjoying the beautiful day. A few skateboarders whizzed by, listening to headphones. Cornelia could practically smell the excitement of summer and the fun days ahead. She loved the feel of her shiny, new medal dangling from around her neck.

"He's more than just a dream," Cornelia explained to Elyon, her voice taking on a more serious tone. It was nice to confide in Elyon about the boy who appeared in her dreams.

Elyon smiled and giggled softly. "I know, Cornelia." She looked at her, her pale blue eyes sparkling. "You've told me so much about him that I feel like I've already met him. But while you're looking for your imaginary prince, you could still hang out with Pete. He's a really great guy."

"No," Cornelia said unequivocally. "I have room for only one great love. And I don't want anyone but him." She held her head high and smiled.

"You really are hopeless," Elyon teased. She reached into one of her skirt pockets and rustled around. "Oh, I have a gift for you," she said.

"A gift for me?" Cornelia repeated, sounding surprised.

The two friends stopped walking. Cornelia looked at Elyon, feeling excited and a little confused.

"To celebrate your skating victory!" Elyon explained. She pulled a white envelope out of her pocket and handed it to Cornelia. "I just knew you'd do well." She looked proudly at her friend.

Cornelia carefully opened the envelope. She pulled out a piece of paper and slowly unfolded a sketch that Elyon had made. She stared, her eyes growing wide in amazement. She couldn't believe what she saw on the page.

It was a drawing of the boy from her dreams. Everything had been captured perfectly – from his handsome face to his dark, disheveled hair to his dreamy, brown eyes and sweet lips. Even his long coat – it was all there.

"Cornelia, does it look like him?" Elyon asked hopefully.

"It's him!" Cornelia cried, her face becoming as bright as a star. "Exactly like in my dreams!" She hugged the drawing to her chest and tried to contain her big, bright smile. Then she leaned over and hugged Elyon. "Thank you," she said. She couldn't have asked for a better gift – or a better friend.

"It's nothing, Cornelia," Elyon replied softly, seemingly overcome with emotion. "You're my best friend."

Cornelia looked down at the sketch again,

admiring the drawing. Then she spotted something written at the bottom of the page in
Elyon's familiar, curly script:

One day you'll meet him, it said. Over the
letter *i*, Elyon had drawn a heart. The picture
was signed *Elyon*.

"It *will* come true someday," Elyon assured
her. "You'll see."

That was then, this is now, Cornelia thought
adamantly, crashing back to reality once again.
She looked around her room sadly and closed
the diary.

"I really wanted it to come true, Ellie," she
whispered quietly. A feeling of sadness made
Cornelia stop and pause. What hurt even more
than never meeting her dream boy was realis-
ing that she and Elyon were no longer friends.
Elyon was now a totally different person. A
stranger!

It was no longer that summer day full of
best-friend bonding; fresh, fragrant grass; the
skating medal; and a thoughtful gift. It was
winter – and the snow was coming down
heavily and creating a thick, icy layer over
Heatherfield. Nothing was the same. And the

air had a chill that made Cornelia shiver.

As Cornelia picked up her blue coat and wrapped it around herself, she braced herself for the cold winter wind – and for her talk with Will. She had to make her understand. There was no other choice.

FOUR

"Ugh!" Will scowled, gaping in disgust at her reflection. She was standing uncomfortably in front of the large, oval mirror in her bedroom, wearing a red, scoop-necked minidress with princess sleeves and an empire waist encircled by a red ribbon. But the worst part of it all? The boots. Made of imitation, brown-and-white leopard skin, they rose to just above her knees and sagged all the way down her legs, leaving odd gaps and pouches.

She felt like a little kid. Knobby knees and a face that looked anything but sophisticated. Her collection of frog-shaped knickknacks, usually a guaranteed picker-upper, wasn't helping, either. It just made her feel that much younger. She was still stewing about

Jackie, the older girl she had met in the pet shop. A driver's licence *and* a sports car? Oooh, was Will jealous.

"Let's change *again*," she moaned to herself. "I want to find something that will leave Matt breathless."

Suddenly, the red dress and boots vanished. Will stood in front of the mirror, staring. For a moment she wore nothing but a magical, pink breeze that swirled around her. What was coming next? she wondered. Almost as though someone had been reading her mind, an entirely new outfit appeared on her body.

This one was no better than the first. It was avocado green with assorted yellow and green dots. Will looked as though she had been pelted with lemons and limes – and they had stuck to the dress' woolly material.

The hideous ensemble was trimmed with fur – tons of it, puffing out from the three-quarter-length sleeves, growing from the collar, and drooping down from the hem. She looked like some sort of crazed animal! Completing the outfit was a pair of high-heeled, strappy, green sandals that wrapped halfway up her legs. The final touch was her hair, which darted out in all directions. She was a fashion disaster!

She was getting frustrated. Why wouldn't her powers just work for her to create the perfect outfit?

"Excuse me, I'm looking for Will," a familiar voice said from the doorway, interrupting her thoughts.

"She's a friend of mine," Cornelia called out, stifling a snort of laughter. "Have you seen her? Or have I ended up at the zoo?"

Will gasped and quickly turned her head, her fists balled up in anger. To prove just how angry she was, she stamped her foot. A maniacal look crossed her face. "Stop joking!" she cried over her shoulder in embarrassment. Did she really look like an animal?

She turned back to the mirror and took another look, relaxing a bit. Maybe the outfit wasn't *so* bad.

"All joking aside, what do you think?" Will asked, a bit more calmly. She turned around so that Cornelia could check out the complete ensemble.

"Do you really want my honest opinion?" Cornelia replied, taking off her blue winter coat.

Will held her breath hopefully and nodded.

Cornelia was superfashionable and always had on the perfect outfit. No one was a better shopper than Cornelia, or kept up better with new fashions. She would definitely be able to help – or at least offer a reliable opinion.

Cornelia looked at Will, assessing her outfit. But her expression could not hide the way she truly felt about Will's choice. Cornelia shut one eye, as if to emphasize her disgust and shield her senses from the bright-green hideousness of Will's ensemble.

"I guess that answers my question," Will said, noting the look on Cornelia's face. "I knew it. It's horrible." And with that, she used her hands once again to cast the pink magic swirls around her body. This time, when the swirls disappeared, Will was in her original clothes – a comfy, orange sweater and pink underpants.

"If you're using your powers to change your look, something must be wrong," Cornelia remarked. "What's up?" She looked at Will quizzically, with bright, understanding blue eyes.

"Hmmm," Will said sheepishly, shrugging her shoulders. She was tempted to tell Cornelia all about Jackie and her stylish outfit, but suddenly she felt quiet and less willing than usual to share. She wasn't sure if Cornelia would understand – especially because Cornelia herself was always so stylish. "I don't want to talk about it."

"Okay, if you say so," Cornelia replied. "However," she added, crossing her arms, "I do need to talk to *you* – about Elyon."

"What about her?" Will asked. She tucked a stray piece of hair behind her ear. Will knew that Cornelia had been hit the hardest by Elyon's odd behavior and by her disappearance. But even though Will knew how hurt Cornelia was, she couldn't overlook the grave fact that Elyon had sided against the Guardians of the Veil.

As Cornelia paced silently around Will's room, Will sat down on the edge of the bed, waiting to hear what she had to say. It wasn't like Cornelia to open up about anything, especially when it came to her thoughts about Elyon. Will wasn't sure where all of this was going. She sat patiently.

Suddenly, Cornelia stopped pacing and stood with her back to Will. Will could tell by her posture that she was serious – and upset.

"Before we became Guardians of the Veil, everything was different. Elyon was different," Cornelia protested.

Will looked up at Corneila with an expectant gaze.

"She was my best friend for so long," Cornelia explained, turning around again to face Will. "I can't believe she has turned into a monster." She took a deep breath and continued. "I want to know why she changed and if there is anything left of the girl I knew. But the only way to do that is to go to Meridian and talk to her, face to face."

Will's eyes grew wide at the thought of Meridian, the immense, magical city within the world of Metamoor that was ruled by the evil Prince Phobos.

Phobos's faithful lieutenant, Lord Cedric, had first taken Elyon to Meridian. And it was there that Elyon had discovered that Phobos was her brother. But Cedric had filled Elyon's head with many lies – including several about her family. He also convinced her that the poverty and suffering in Metamoor was to be blamed on the Guardians.

Under Cedric's spell, Elyon had deceived

the Guardians many times – causing them on more than one occasion to end up in fairly intense Metamoorian battles. And even though Will and her friends had real-deal, awesome powers, Metamoor was still a scary place.

Now, as far as Will was concerned, Elyon was nothing but trouble. She looked down at her feet and realised she had unconsciously been kicking the dust ruffle. At times like these, Will really felt the pressure and the responsibility of holding the Heart of Candracar within her. She was the leader of the team – a most reluctant leader, but, even so – chosen to unite the force of the Guardians' powers.

While she understood that Cornelia wanted to go and see Elyon, she didn't think it was a wise decision. After a few minutes of silence, she managed to mutter, "It's a crazy idea. And you know it."

Cornelia shot Will a startled look, her blonde eyebrows knit in a perplexed frown. Will could see how hurt Cornelia was and how miserable she was feeling. She wished that she had the power to help her friend – or even that she knew the right thing to say to her. But she was not sure about Elyon and her role in the Meridian mess.

While their Guardian powers allowed the girls to do many things, there was a limit. And so, Will was powerless as she watched Cornelia silently get up and leave.

FIVE

Feeling lost and confused, Cornelia walked slowly past the Sheffield Institute. Snow was still falling heavily, but she had her red umbrella open to protect her from the giant flakes. She pulled up the collar of her blue winter coat to shield her neck from the freezing wind. Even through the coat she felt a chill, but it wasn't caused by cold winter air – it was caused by despair.

She went over the conversation with Will in her head. Of course, Will doesn't understand, she thought. After all, she's only seen the worst side of Elyon. She doesn't know Elyon like the rest of us do. But Irma and Hay Lin knew the old Elyon. They must remember how she acted before this whole ordeal. She was a good friend and a sweet girl.

Cornelia marched quickly towards the park behind the school. She headed that way, knowing Irma and Hay Lin would be there, for their extra-credit biology session with Mrs. Vargas.

I'm sure they will understand what I'm feeling. They must remember how things used to be around here, Cornelia thought as she walked through the snowy streets.

She spotted Irma and Hay Lin right away among the other students. Most of the students were busy snapping photos for their extra-credit session. They were pointing and clicking, taking artsy shots of icicles and footprints – not an easy task with mittens on. Mrs. Vargas stood in the distance beside a few of the students, holding her purse in one hand and pointing purposefully with the other.

Cornelia saw Irma and Hay Lin huddled together a few steps away from the group. They weren't taking pictures yet. Cornelia made her way over to her friends, careful not to disrupt the session. As her friends began to focus and shoot their photos of the icy landscape, Cornelia launched into an explanation of what was upsetting her. She told them everything:

how she felt about Elyon, and how she couldn't believe that their friend had changed into such a horrible person. She wanted to make Irma and Hay Lin remember when they had been friends with Elyon. She explained that she wanted to go to Metamoor to find out if there was anything about Elyon that was still the same.

"Very good idea, Corny," said Irma, who couldn't resist doing things like using a silly nickname to get under Cornelia's skin. "If you want Cedric's musclemen to attack you, that's the perfect solution."

Cornelia hated to admit it, but she saw Irma's point. Cedric was sly, vicious, and completely evil. He had lured Elyon back to Metamoor by telling her a distorted version of her past so that he could keep her under his control. The thought of meeting up with him was not appealing. Cedric was pure evil. Still, she had to do something. She couldn't just sit around any longer.

"Irma's right," said Hay Lin, who looked, to Cornelia, a bit like a blue marshmallow in her puffy winter coat. Hay Lin had her own style and wore unique clothes – including funky goggles on top of her head. Often, her clothes were not at all Cornelia's style. But Cornelia had to hand it to Hay Lin for having her own offbeat look.

"Never mind," Cornelia huffed. "I get it. You don't agree." As she wrapped her arms across her body for extra warmth, she felt superdisappointed. Why weren't her friends being more understanding?

"I just wouldn't want to take a vacation in the Metamoor prison," Irma said drily. "Would you?" She elbowed Hay Lin gently in the ribs, and they each let out a giggle.

That's it! Cornelia thought. I've had enough. Clearly, Irma and Hay Lin are not taking this seriously!

She had no other choice. Cornelia knew what she had to do, and she knew just how to do it. Taking off, she ran down the sidewalk, her long coat, ankle-length skirt, and blonde hair billowing out behind her.

"Cornelia!" she heard Hay Lin call out after her. "Stop! Wait!" But Cornelia was determined. She was on a mission – and nothing, not even her fellow Guardians, could stop her. She was going to have to go solo on this adventure. And the adventure had to start now.

"Wait!" Hay Lin cried again as she started to run after Cornelia.

"Hay Lin!" Mrs. Vargas called out from behind her. "Hay Lin!"

Turning to look over her shoulder, Cornelia saw Hay Lin stop in her tracks, turn, and face Mrs. Vargas.

Mrs. Vargas had one hand on her hip and was pointing with the other towards the roof of a nearby shed lined with icicles. "Look out for those stalactites! Observe the solidification process of the water, and then take a picture of it!" she ordered.

"Grrr!" Hay Lin muttered to herself. "Yes, ma'am," she said to her teacher with a polite smile. Hay Lin unhooked the little camera that was hanging from her wrist and then zoomed in on the ice formation.

Irma trotted over to the shed and stood next to Hay Lin. Following Mrs. Vargas' directions, they both got up close to the shed to focus on their photographic subject.

They lifted their cameras up to their faces and glanced slyly at each other. There was nothing they could do – Mrs. Vargas had commanded, and they had to obey.

Cornelia knew that the two girls were concerned about her and were wondering if she
could travel to Meridian alone, without Will
and the Heart of Candracar and without the
power of the other four girls. Cornelia was having the same thoughts.

I have to go, even if I have to go alone, she
decided. Hurrying down the street through
the blinding snowstorm, she stopped at an
ordinary-looking store window and paused.
She glanced up at the icicle-covered sign above
the window – *Ye Olde Bookshop*, it said. This
was the place. This unassuming bookstore was
where it had all started. It was where Elyon had
had her first date with Cedric – and it was the
site of her disappearance.

Reaching for the big, brass doorknob,
Cornelia carefully turned it. The door opened
with a creak. Poking her head into the store,
she got a whiff of that musty, old, leathery,
book smell. The room was dark and shadowy –
just as she remembered it. She slowly stepped inside and let the door close behind
her. Feeling as if she were in an old movie,
Cornelia took a deep breath and tried not

to be creeped out by the old, spooky store.

"Anyone in here?" Cornelia hollered, inching her way further into the store. She could hear a rustling sound coming from somewhere in the back. Apparently, she was not alone. "Whoever you are," she demanded, "come out now."

Cornelia crept slowly along, her hands stretched out in front of her. The whole place felt abandoned and eerie. Tall, dusty bookcases surrounded her, and books lay scattered on the floor. She noticed that some shelves were practically empty – and others appeared to have been knocked over.

"Come on," she called out again. "I know you're there."

Wait, what was that? she wondered. She could have sworn she had heard a creaky noise coming from behind a big, wooden desk. Her heartbeat quickened.

Who was that? Was it Cedric? Or was it another one of the evil creatures sent from Metamoor to attack the Guardians?

She rested her hand on the desk and peered around. Then . . .

"You!" she gasped. Cornelia's eyes widened

in disbelief, and the hairs on the back of her neck stood up. "Vathek!"

Standing in front of her was a very large, very blue-faced monster. It was Cedric's right-hand man – the creature who carried out Cedric's evil commands, which usually involved doing something harmful to Cornelia and her friends.

"I wasn't looking forward to this – to finding you here," he growled. He stared at her with his deep-set eyes, and he bared razor-sharp fangs. Suddenly, he reached out an extra-large, blue claw in her direction. She recoiled in horror.

She quickly closed her eyes and concentrated. This was no time to be just a girl. She needed all the strength she could muster. She felt the familiar whoosh of green whirling around her body, and an electric thrill tingled down her spine. Her body grew taller and stronger, pulsating with power. Leafy wings emerged from her back, making her feel weightless. The swirls disappeared. She had successfully transformed herself into the magical Cornelia. She was now feeling the strength and power of a Guardian of the Veil.

"Get ready to fight with the powers of the

earth!" she announced boldly. She stood poised and ready to take the creature on.

"I won't fight you," Vathek said calmly, turning his hulking, blue body from Cornelia and retreating.

Cornelia couldn't believe what she was hearing. "What?" She asked. She was shocked – and almost disappointed. With the power of earth inside her, she was convinced she could battle Vathek and win. The enormous blue creature stepped back into a dark corner, and Cornelia followed. She was not afraid. She was ready to fight.

Behind a bookcase that was knocked over, Vathek was sitting on the floor, picking up a few of the fallen books. He placed them carefully in a pile. "I know what Cedric has done," he said as Cornelia approached him.

"What do you mean?" Cornelia asked, still unsure of the blue beast. She knelt next to him, surprised to hear him speak negatively about his boss.

Cornelia needed some answers. Perhaps this blue creature could give her some information. He seemed to not be aligned with Cedric anymore. "Have you betrayed him?"

"I just opened my eyes," he replied, staring into the distance. Then he stood up again, holding a book in his clawlike hand. He placed it back on a shelf. From the spot on the floor where Cornelia hovered, Vathek looked gigantic. "My people have suffered too long at the hands of Phobos. Now, I'm determined to help those who fight against Phobos – to bring joy and peace back to Meridian."

Cornelia watched him with curiosity as he went about collecting several pieces of paper from around the shop. It was very strange. He didn't look nearly as menacing as she remembered. He actually looked kind of sweet, and almost gentle.

"Good," he said, looking down at the papers in his hands. "I have everything Caleb asked for."

"Caleb . . ." The name made Cornelia stop and think. What was this strange reaction she was feeling? She fell into a minitrance. Caleb. Caleb. Caleb – she repeated the name in her mind. She scratched her forehead, unsure why the mention of that name would have such an impact on her.

What's happening to me? she wondered.

That name . . . just the sound of it sent warm energy fluttering through her body, as if she had had a deep connection to the person. The name seemed so familiar.

Then it hit her. That feeling. That boy. She had felt this before – in her dreams.

It's not possible! she thought, shaking off the cloud of confusion that had engulfed her.

Suddenly, she heard a loud *clang* behind her. Vathek had flung aside a bookcase. Cracks were spreading throughout the brick wall behind it, and a few chunks of plaster had fallen to the floor. The big blue creature was descending through an opening in the floor that had previously been hidden. A bright shaft of light rose up out of it, brightening the room.

"Goodbye, young Guardian," Vathek said, smiling up kindly at Cornelia. He descended farther, deep into the glowing hole beneath the bookshop.

"Wait!" she cried. "Take me with you!" She held out her hand, her eyes pleading with him. Not waiting for a response, she crawled through the secret entrance and found herself on a circular staircase. The place was dark and damp. She held onto the wall to brace herself.

Luckily, Vathek, who was only a few paces ahead, had a torch. The bright flame cast a golden light throughout the stairwell. "If you have changed, maybe Elyon has changed too. . ." she said.

"Mmm . . . don't count on it," said Vathek. "She is a slave to Cedric."

Cornelia refused to believe that Elyon was really evil and wanted to be with someone as cruel and coldhearted as Cedric. There had to be a reason for all these sudden changes in Elyon's personality. And now that Vathek was being so helpful, everything had become even more confusing. She had no choice but to follow this creature to find out more.

Cornelia traveled with the blue creature through the tunnel, wondering what she would find ahead.

The two continued to walk carefully down the dark tunnel, side by side. What a pair we must make, Cornelia thought, as she tried to keep up with Vathek's fast pace: a tall, slim girl and a gigantic, blue monster with an enormous torso.

"Well, I guess we can hope," Vathek said encouragingly as he led the way to Meridian.

"Who knows? Maybe Elyon *has* changed."

And so they journeyed towards Meridian together, each lost in thought. Thinking about her fellow Guardians' thoughts and fears, Cornelia slowly moved forward.

Each of us needs to find courage for each of our individual problems, Cornelia realised. How strange that all of our lives are so connected. We each have struggles within our lives in Heatherfield, but now we need to think about the people of Meridian as well. But Cornelia was determined to find just one person in Meridian – Elyon – and save her.

SIX

Outside the city of Meridian, Elyon walked with Cedric down a narrow path in a dark forest. The tree branches were like thick vines that twisted upward, and there were electric-green, pointy-leaved plants that shimmered against the enormous, aquamarine sky. The pair were surrounded by the vermilion-coloured mushrooms and dark roses that bloomed everywhere. Everything was quiet – which made the forest a perfect place to have a private conversation.

She and Cedric made a funny couple, Elyon thought as they walked. Cedric sauntered along in his reptile form, his scaly, green skin, muscular chest, sharp teeth, and thick, serpentine tail making a sharp contrast with Elyon's fine, petite features. His hair hung long down his back. It was greyish, rather than the light blond colour it possessed when Cedric was in human form.

Elyon wore a loose, blue dress with a large, striped, silver-blue shawl. She held her brown cloak draped over her arm; her mouth was turned down in a grimace of frustration and confusion.

"Nothing makes sense anymore," Elyon said. "I don't understand what is going on." She took a deep breath and pleaded with the snake-man. "Cedric, will you tell me what is happening?"

"Try to be quiet," Cedric scolded. His beady eyes peered out from behind his slimy, red mask.

"No! Explain yourself!" shouted Elyon. "You attacked Will after she saved your life! Why?"

The memory of what had happened made her blood boil. She recalled the scene, remembering how Cedric had actually tried to harm Will after she had performed a kind, generous act and saved his life. Battles like these were becoming too frequent – and too dangerous. Nothing made any sense.

Elyon was beginning to have some serious doubts about Cedric. She had believed him when he first took her to Meridian, though what he had told her about her friends didn't quite add up, but now . . . She looked up at the green creature who was more than twice her size. How could he have tried to hurt Will? "It's shameful behavior for anybody," she said angrily.

"Ha-ha-ha!" Cedric laughed. "Grow up, little girl!" He leaned down and curled his large claws menacingly. "You cannot think like a little girl anymore." He casually wrapped his long tail around her back and snarled. "You are a princess. The Princess of Meridian."

"If you say so," she said, holding up her hand to signal Cedric to stop speaking. "In that case, I order you to leave me alone." She turned and began to walk away from him.

"Where are you going?" Cedric demanded. He had not expected that response from Elyon.

"I want to see Meridian," Elyon said over her shoulder. "Alone." She put on her brown cloak, sticking her arms through the loose sleeves. "I need to understand why people leave this place," she continued, pulling the hood up over her head to hide her face. Her long, blonde braids hung straight down in front of her chest. "I need to find the cause of all the pain here."

She walked out of the forest and stepped onto a stone ledge that looked down over the city of Meridian. There were stone-lined streets and old-fashioned stone buildings. Off in the distance she saw the Royal Palace. If there hadn't been such heavy despair and gloom surrounding the city, it would have been a glorious place, Elyon thought sadly. She felt small, gazing out at the vast village spread out before her.

The smell of smoke filled the air. Something was burning, she thought. Suddenly, large flames burst from a building in front of her.

She turned her attention to what was happening below and gasped. A house was on fire! Two soldiers in grey-and-blue uniforms had set the blaze with burning sticks. Smoke billowed from the scene, sending a mile-long trail wafting over the gloomy village.

Her eyes drifted to a group of villagers. They had turned their backs on the burning house; their shoulders sagged. Elyon could tell they were sad and ashamed. Some were coughing from the smoke. The people of the city seemed to have given up hope.

Elyon moved closer to the town and listened to the voices rising. She heard a little boy ask his parents, "Why did the guard burn our house?" He looked frightened, and Elyon's heart ached for him.

"Don't ask questions, little one," his father answered as the three of them stood by, watching helplessly.

Again the boy piped up. "Mummy says it's the fault of Phob – " Before the boy could finish his sentence, the father quickly placed his hand over the boy's mouth. It was obvious he was afraid the child would be harmed if he said the prince's name.

"Don't say another word," he cautioned the boy. Silently, they watched as orange-and-yellow flames engulfed their house.

Elyon had now moved down even closer to the villagers, her big hood shielding her face. As the crowd surged forward, she shuffled down to the street and stood beside them.

Phobos, my brother, she thought with disdain. If he is responsible for this destruction, he must be stopped.

SEVEN

Phobos, the cruel and powerful prince of Meridian, stood tall and menacing in his blue-and-white, flowing robes. His long, blond braids hung down practically to his ankles. A crown, ornamented with a ridged, turquoise triangle adorned his head. And his eyes were intense, focused, and distant.

Before him stood his faithful henchman, Cedric. Leaning forward on his hands, Cedric hunched over in deference. His tail was curled up close against his strong, green body. He waited for Phobos' response to Elyon's escape, and to the news of her walking the streets of Meridian alone.

"Why did you let her go?" Phobos asked coldly, rays of severe, blue light shooting out from his body in every direction. He stood still and waited for an answer.

Cedric remained silent for a moment, drained of his usual strength.

"Answer me!" Phobos commanded. The bright light reflecting off the red jewels that decorated Phobos' forehead nearly blinded Cedric.

Phobos was growing impatient, and Cedric seemed to be faltering. There was no time for mistakes, and no room for error. He glared at Cedric, willing him to answer immediately.

"I thank you for honouring me with your presence," Cedric finally said. "And I'm willing to explain everything."

Phobos noticed that Cedric's face appeared much paler and weaker in the flood of bright light than it had before.

"Your sister is unsure and doubtful of her feelings," Cedric continued gravely. "She needs to be confident of her role if she is fully to acquire her powers."

"Make her realise soon," the tyrant said icily, in a near-whisper, "that she must not become a symbol for the rebellion." He gazed at Cedric with a gritty stare. Did Cedric not realise the urgency of the situation? Did he not know what was at stake? "I need to absorb her as soon as possible," Phobos finished, a barely noticeable scowl flitting across his face. His perfect plan was almost in place. Nothing could get in his way now – not even his sister.

EIGHT

Water was swirling all around Cornelia. Powerful currents thrust her forward with a force she had never felt before. All the other times she had gone to Metamoor, she had been with the other Guardians. This time, she was alone. And she was scared.

She felt herself flying through a deep, curved channel. It was cold. She was having serious doubts about her decision. What was she thinking, trying to go to Meridian without her friends?

Cornelia missed Irma and her ability to calm the water. She missed Taranee, for her control of fire, and Hay Lin for her bursts of soothing air. And she missed Will, for her strength and for the Heart of Candracar.

Trying to slow her panicked breathing, Cornelia held her breath for a few seconds and then exhaled slowly. Calm, stay calm, she thought. She wasn't sure when she had accidentally let go of Vathek's hand. Somewhere on their journey to Metamoor they had been separated.

Now, she was totally out of control. It felt as if she were falling sideways.

Nooo! Cornelia thought, horrified. I can't do this without my friends!

Her heart was beating rapidly. She had never felt so frightened and alone before.

"I . . . can't . . . swim!" she whimpered aloud, falling deeper and deeper under the water. The current was even stronger now. Reaching out with her left hand, she tried to paddle, but she had no strength. And the more frightened she became, the weaker she felt. Bubbles rose up around her. She felt her body go limp.

Suddenly, she heard a faint splash above her. She felt a gentle tug. Someone was grabbing her wrist. Up, up, up towards the light, she was being pulled, towards air. "Ahhh!" she gasped, finally breaking through the surface of the water.

She sagged, her body shaking. Coughing, she felt her arms gently pulled higher and higher. She was being lifted up, out of the water, out of danger. She looked over at the strange-looking pool from which she had just emerged. It looked like half of a gigantic oyster shell. Water poured over the sides. In the center of the fountain, a menacing, reptilian sculpture shot water through its mouth.

Cornelia felt dizzy as she tried to figure out her surroundings. Looking around, she saw what looked like a palace, with enormous columns and arches. She could hear voices around her and a crowd off in the distance.

As her head started to clear, Cornelia heard a voice that was familiar. It was Vathek's.

"I don't know what happened. I lost her somewhere along the way," he said, explaining to someone what had happened during his journey with Cornelia.

Then she heard another, more soothing and calming, voice. "Well, she made it out," the voice said. "That's the important thing." After a moment, she realised that the voice came from the person who had rescued her – the same person who was now holding her in his strong arms.

Cornelia slowly turned her head and looked up – at the beautiful boy who held her. *I can't believe it!* she thought. She slowly reached out to stroke his cheek, to make sure he was real. She studied his smooth skin and piercing, green eyes. She could sense his warm, lovable spirit – it was an instant, intense connection.

"You're safe now," he said sweetly, his arm resting protectively around her back, support-ing her.

He cannot really exist, she said to herself, still in a state of disbelief. This cannot be hap-pening. She gazed up at his bright face and charming eyes.

It *was* him: the boy of her dreams. The one she had dreamed about for so long and had described to Elyon so clearly. She let out a sigh. She had finally found him. And he was even dreamier in person!

"Who is that?" she heard someone say, obviously pointing at her. Half a dozen eyes were staring at her, invading her special moment with her dream boy. The creatures – all varying shades of green – crowded around the two of them. And the creatures were getting a bit unruly.

"She's not one of us," one said snootily, shaking a finger at Cornelia.

"She can't stay here," said another.

"And she's ugly," added a shorter one, who was covered in orange spots.

This last comment was too much for Cornelia. *They* were calling *her* ugly? She knew that she was waterlogged and had just nearly drowned, but, come on! She couldn't control her anger. "Have you looked in the mirror lately?" she snapped peevishly at the creature who had made the remark.

"She'll bring us problems," another Meridian native advised, ignoring her outburst completely.

"Be quiet, all of you!" Cornelia's saviour said, trying to calm everyone down. "I can vouch for her."

He is truly dreamy, Cornelia thought. It was obvious that he was in charge, and that he needed to keep the creatures calm. But Cornelia liked the fact that he was sticking up for her.

She remembered what Vathek had said, and

she quickly pieced the situation together. These were the Meridian people who were rebelling against Prince Phobos – and against the years of lies, poverty, and suffering the Metamoorians had had to endure under his rule. This boy was the rebels' fearless leader. She gazed at him admiringly.

"Caleb!" shouted a shaggy creature who had just raced up from behind them. He looked as though he were about to faint from fear. "They're coming!"

Cornelia gasped. The boy's name was Caleb! Now she knew why she had had such a strong reaction when Vathek had said his name earlier.

Vathek ran over and protectively threw his big, blue arms around the shaggy fellow. "It's the end!" he shouted, fear creeping into his voice.

Cornelia felt fearful. If Vathek, this large, strong creature, was afraid, she had to wonder. What was going on here?

"The soldiers spotted us," the newly arrived creature continued. He was in a great panic. "They're about to attack!"

"It's hopeless," cried a rebel with pointy,

green ears. He shook his head from side to side.

"I knew it," said another.

Cornelia looked at Caleb's face, waiting to see what he would do. He didn't look as though he thought it were either the end *or* time to give up.

One of the monsters glared over Caleb's shoulder at Cornelia. It was the sour-faced, orange-spotted one again – the one who had insulted Cornelia a few moments earlier. It seemed he wasn't quite done yet. He clearly didn't like her. "I knew you'd bring us problems," he said.

"Stop it," Cornelia retorted angrily, her hands in fists at her sides. She was starting to get a little peeved at this guy.

Caleb stepped up and took charge. His voice was calm and firm. "Vathek!" he commanded, pointing forcefully at the large, blue creature. "Take one group with you. The others will follow me."

"Right," Vathek said, nodding his head. He seemed willing to do anything that Caleb wanted him to do. Cornelia found herself looking at Caleb with even more respect than before.

Putting a hand on Cornelia's shoulder, Caleb led her through an archway. "Come on, let's go," he said to her.

The touch of Caleb's hand was comforting, and she realised he made her feel safe. They pushed forward together through the crowds and made their way towards the front of the group.

The Metamoorian rebels followed behind them. Cornelia heard the sound of hundreds of the palace guards' boots pounding against the stone floor of a bridge above her. Her Guardian senses were kicking in.

"They're close!" Cornelia called out anxiously. "I can feel it."

"We'll never make it!" a rebel shouted fearfully from behind them.

"Quick!" someone else cried frantically. "They can't catch us!"

Cornelia stopped at a stone balcony to look out on the city. She gazed down at the front of the palace wall, which was covered in a mass of thick, red leaves and vines.

Suddenly, a voice caught her attention. It came from down below. "Leave me alone!" a girl's voice called out. That voice, thought

Cornelia. It sounded so familiar. Could it be . . . ? It was. . . *Elyon*!

Cornelia watched the scene from the top of the castle. Elyon looked small among the massive soldiers with their blue, padded uniforms, sharp weapons, and white spikes that sprouted from their faces. They surrounded her, but Elyon appeared defiant and strong.

"They're escaping!" a guard cried out, pointing up to the rebels gathering at the top of the palace. "Surround the building!" he shouted. He smashed his sword furiously into the ground.

Another soldier made his way over to Elyon. He must have been the leader, because he was the only one with a gold medallion displayed on his breastplate. He rested one hand on his hip. With the other, he reached out to grasp the glowing green pendant that Elyon wore around her neck.

"Since when do runts like you wear precious jewels?" he asked menacingly. He was a big beast with hair pulled back into a bun on the top of his head, exposing wide jowls and an angry expression.

"Remove your hand, and apologise, you big

monkey!" Elyon commanded, casting upon him her meanest look. "I am Princess Elyon!" She grabbed back her necklace.

"Ha-ha-ha!" he laughed. "And I am a little butterfly," he said, mocking Elyon.

"Arrest her!" he said to one of his large henchmen. Then, before you could say "ugly fangs," he tugged at the green jewel around Elyon's neck. With a quick *snap* it came loose. Simultaneously, another guard pinned both of her arms behind her.

"Let me go," Elyon screamed. *"Nooo!"* A burly, red-bearded guard with giant hands started to lead her away. "Phobos will make you pay!" she shouted at the guard.

"Suuure!" sneered the necklace-stealer. "He always punishes us when we follow his orders." He held up the glowing, green jewel in his claw to admire it, and laughed loudly. "Take her away with the others," he ordered. "Then follow me."

"Let me go," Elyon shouted again. But it was no use. Two guards were pulling her by the arms. "I'm Elyon!" she protested. "I'm the princess. . . ."

Elyon stopped struggling. She looked weak

and sad. Her eyes were heavy, and her head hung low. She was losing all her strength and will to fight.

Cornelia couldn't take any more. She no longer could bear to stand by and watch without doing something.

"And I am her ex–best friend!" Cornelia shouted, landing in a perfect crouching-tiger position in front of Elyon and the guards. She had jumped all the way down from the top of the palace. She was ready to battle this beast and save her friend.

The guards were so surprised by Cornelia's sudden appearance that they let go of their grip on the prisoner.

"Cornelia!" Elyon cried out with delight and admiration. For a moment, Cornelia saw a glimmer of Elyon's old self in her expression.

Quickly, Cornelia summoned up some healthy earth power and let it pulse through her. A green light encircled her body as power surged all around her.

Now energised, she stroked a cluster of the red leaves that covered the palace walls. The green power oozed forth from her hand, causing several long branches instantly to grow out – horizontally.

Then, Cornelia reached out towards a near-by tree, breaking off a branch. She quickly lassoed the branch and wrapped it like a belt five times around the guard's waist. She flung him high into the air.

"Aaargh!" the guard wailed as he dangled above them.

Elyon appeared startled. "What are you doing here?" she asked Cornelia, letting out a sigh of relief. "You're the last person I expected to see."

Cornelia didn't have time to respond. She had spotted three brutes barreling towards them. A green vapour began seeping up from the floor, causing it to crack.

"What do you think about postponing this chat for now and helping me out?" Cornelia asked. She leaned forward on her knees, arched her back, and extended her arms out in front of her.

"Help!" screamed one of the approaching guards, as he slipped on some green slime.

"Stop them!" shouted another soldier, scurrying closer to Elyon and Cornelia.

"Now what will we do?" screamed Elyon.

"Join forces!" Cornelia cried. Elyon nodded in silent agreement.

The two stood side by side and extended their hands, palms up.

"Powers of the earth," Cornelia commanded, beckoning her magic energy.

Elyon bent her head and concentrated. "Well," she said, "I don't know which power this is, but I hope it works!"

Together, the girls' forces created a dynamic ray and an earsplitting *zooot!* Swirls of green and blue light flashed and then shot out towards the guards. Their aim was perfect.

"Run!" cried one of the soldiers, lurching heavily backward. He looked terrified. The other guards went crashing to the ground.

"Move!" one shouted.

"Help!" screamed another, his sword falling from his hand.

Ruuuumble!

Cornelia and Elyon suddenly felt an intense vibration beneath them. They stopped in their tracks, lowering their hands. Their powers together were a real force. A rolling motion began happening all around them.

Ruuuumble!

"What did we do?" Elyon cried out.

"Oops . . ." Cornelia said, wiping her brow. "Maybe that was a little too much."

Waves from the earth continued to travel speedily in all directions – shaking and jerking and rolling around.

Then, right before their eyes, the gigantic stone building collapsed and came crashing down. Thick slabs of stone crumbled all around them.

"Oh, no!" Elyon shrieked. "What have we done?"

Cornelia grabbed Elyon's hand and ran.

NINE

The Oracle – the benevolent, all-knowing being who had anointed the five Guardians of the Veil – meditated in the sacred Temple of Candracar.

The Temple of Candracar was still and peaceful, suspended in a silvery substance that was lighter than air and purer than water. It was the very center of all of the magical worlds – a mystical palace in the middle of infinity. Its residents, mighty, powerful spirits and creatures, protected the harmony of the universe.

The Oracle gazed down peacefully at the town of Heatherfield. Checking in on the other Guardians, he watched as the mighty burst of power created in Meridian by Cornelia and Elyon made its effect felt in Heatherfield.

Broooaam!

He continued to watch as Irma and Hay Lin huddled tightly together in the park with their teacher close by.

"Students . . . stay calm!" Mrs. Vargas shouted, catching a student who had stumbled into her arms. "It's only a little shake!" she said, trying to remain in control and cheerful.

"A little shake?" Irma whispered to Hay Lin, her eyes practically popping out of her head.

"I think Mrs. Vargas is just trying to reassure us," Hay Lin replied, throwing her arms tightly around Irma.

Finally, the Oracle turned his attention towards Will, who was at home and about to step into the shower. When the floor started shaking and the walls began rattling, she lost her balance and tumbled to the ground. Her feet went out from underneath her, and she landed on the blue-tiled floor – and right on her bottom. Her toothpaste, hairbrush, lotions, shampoo, mug, and a wicker laundry basket all came crashing down around her.

She sat up shakily in her white terry-cloth

robe and looked around. "What's going on?" she asked out loud.

The Oracle left the Guardians and sat meditating in a lotus pose, floating effortlessly on a current of air. Lilies floated beneath him in a pool of serene water. He remained calm, even though the scenes below showed chaos and uncertainty.

Two council members stood nearby: Luba, the catlike council member who was sometimes tough in her assessments and always skeptical of the Guardians, and Tibor, the Oracle's faithful adviser, who was always ready to obey. They, too, observed the events that had transpired in Meridian and Heatherfield.

"They shouldn't have done that," Luba said with a low growl after she witnessed Cornelia and Elyon releasing their combined powers in Meridian. "They have unleashed dark forces!" Her voice was full of concern and contempt, and her anger was growing.

"By joining forces, Cornelia and Elyon have opened another portal in the Veil," Tibor muttered, stroking his long, white beard. He looked worried. The Veil was very fragile, and the Council of the Congregation didn't want any more portals to be opened up. "Earth and Metamoor are in great danger!" he continued, his eyes growing even wider.

"The Guardians are not up to this task!" Luba snarled, her whiskers poking out like a porcupine's. She was still worried that the Oracle had put too much faith in those five young girls.

"Hush," said the Oracle, as trusting as ever in his Guardians. "Let destiny take its course." His face remained full of a Zen-like calm, and his infinite wisdom allowed him to believe in the good of the universe – to understand and accept others' uncertainties and feelings.

The Oracle tapped his finger on the pool, creating a gentle vibration. The sound echoed throughout the Temple. Slowly, a vision of Elyon and Cornelia appeared in the watery ripples of the sacred pool.

"Let the girls find their own way," he instructed. "And you must find your trust in them."

TEN

Irma hurried along the snowy streets on her way to meet her friends. Everything seemed extra quiet after the strange and unexpected earthquake and the heavy snowstorm. Now, the city was peaceful, blanketed in a cocoon of white snow.

When Irma saw Taranee and Hay Lin standing outside of Hay Lin's family restaurant, she picked up her pace.

The Silver Dragon was located right under Hay Lin's house – making it quite convenient for her parents to go to work every day.

As Irma walked up to her friends she caught a delicious whiff of garlic-and-ginger chicken coming from the kitchen inside.

"We were so scared," Irma heard Taranee say to Hay Lin as she walked up to the two of them.

Irma knew that Taranee must have been referring to the strange earthquake the day before.

"Scared?" Irma replied breezily as she joined her two friends. "Why? It was only a little earthquake. At least there were no monsters involved." She held up her hands like claws and let out a mean growl. The girls had been in much scarier situations than that old earthquake, Irma mused. Meridian baddies were much more frightening than a few shakes of the earth.

Hay Lin broke out in a fit of giggles as Irma growled. Her laughter made Taranee relax, and she laughed as well.

"Compared to our other experiences," continued Irma, "nothing should upset us." She held her hand to her chest dramatically. Irma loved to take center stage, and this was too good an opportunity to miss.

"I guess so," said Hay Lin. Then, out of nowhere, she began stuttering. "L – l – look . . ." Her voice trailed off.

Irma stared at her stammering friend. Hay Lin was spacing out! "Um . . . looks like there was a lot more damage from that earthquake than we predicted!" she said, raising an eyebrow at Hay Lin, who appeared to have gone a little crazy.

"L – l – look . . ." Hay Lin babbled again, her voice trailing off. But this time, she pointed down the street, attempting to give the others a bit of a clue as to what she was trying to say.

Irma wondered what Hay Lin was talking about. Perhaps the earthquake had shaken Hay Lin up more than she realised. Or, maybe, she had fallen and bumped her head. Irma gave Hay Lin a suspicious look.

"It's not me who's gone crazy," Hay Lin cried, finally able to speak. "Look!"

Hay Lin grabbed Irma by the shoulders and quickly turned her around. And Taranee, adjusting her glasses, slowly turned to see what Hay Lin was pointing at.

"Aaaagh!" Irma screamed, her eyes seeming to pop out of her head. Hay Lin *was* totally fine – it was another Guardian who had been drastically affected by the earthquake!

Irma's gaze fell on her friend Will – or

someone resembling Will. It certainly was Will's sweet face she saw, but the outfit was far from typical for Will. Irma couldn't believe what she was seeing. *Was* that really Will? She looked to Hay Lin and Taranee to gauge their reactions. They all caught one another's eye and tried to hold back their giggles.

Irma turned to face Will and to inspect the new look she was sporting. Irma had to admit that it was a serious attempt at sophistication: a belly-revealing, front-zippered turtleneck; a wraparound miniskirt and tassel belt; a long, cream-coloured coat; and a blue shoulder bag. Although Irma had to admire the clothes, the whole ensemble seemed completely out of character for Will.

Will flashed a small, shy smile and waved at the group.

She must have seen someone else wear that outfit, Irma thought. She looks much older and more sophisticated than usual. I wonder why she wants to dress that way, Irma mused. Maybe she was forced into this new look by some hyper–fashion police in Meridian!

The thought made Irma giggle. "Tell us the truth," she remarked with a squeal. "You were held hostage by a band of crazed stylists, right?"

"Hmmm . . ." Taranee said, with an exaggerated intake of breath. "I smell a date."

"Just like Taranee's with Nigel," Hay Lin teased, giving Taranee a little squeeze. "But unlike Taranee, Will still hasn't told us who her date is."

"I never said I went out with Nigel," Taranee snapped, her cheeks growing pink with embarrassment. Irma smiled – sometimes Taranee could be very predictable.

"You forget I'm a witch?" Hay Lin cackled, wrinkling her face and extending her fingers like claws.

Will stood between her friends, looking decidedly uncomfortable.

Normally, Irma loved to tease her friend Taranee, but right now she was more interested in the new Will and her transformation than in Taranee's so-called date. Where did Will get those clothes, anyway? Irma wondered. They looked strangely familiar. She gave Will an inquisitive look. "So?" she said. She had a sneaking suspicion that something big was going on. "What's the story?"

They all looked expectantly at Will.

"It's nothing special," Will replied, obviously trying to cover something up. She scratched her head, but her hair was so loaded up with gel and hair spray that not one piece of hair moved.

Irma could tell that Will had something on her mind. Was it a vision of someone else wearing the same outfit? Why did Will want to dress differently and in such a sophisticated style? That wasn't like her at all.

"I just wanted to try a new look," Will innocently explained to her friends.

"Well, honestly," Hay Lin said, giving Will a head-to-toe stare. "It's definitely new."

"You don't look like Will," Irma piped up.

"Good. That was the point," Will replied, touching her head to make sure the hairstyle was still holding.

"Let's talk about something else," Irma suggested, sensing Will's discomfort. "Why was this meeting so important, Hay Lin?"

"Oh! I almost forgot about it," Hay Lin said. "I just got a little sidetracked!" She slapped her head with her hand. "Luckily, I have my hands." She held out her palm, showing her friends where she had written the word *map* in fresh, blue ink.

Irma knew her friend well and immediately recognised Hay Lin's classic trick for remembering important things. Hay Lin had a habit of writing notes down on her hand so she wouldn't forget what she had to do. Unfortunately, the arty girl, when she slapped her hand to her forehead, had imprinted the note on her head as well!

"And your forehead!" Irma said casually, pointing to a spot just below Hay Lin's hairline. The letters "M-A-P" were printed backward on Hay Lin's forehead.

The four friends erupted in a fit of laughter. Irma looked at Will and was glad to see that she was laughing along with them. She might have looked different, but she was still the same old Will.

Laughing, Hay Lin wiped the ink from her forehead and led her friends into the restaurant.

The map she had referred to was a gift from her grandmother, who had once been a Guardian of the Veil, too. Hay Lin's grandmother had entrusted her with the map of the twelve portals before she died. The portals provided access to the passageways leading to Metamoor. Though her grandmother had passed away, Hay Lin still felt deeply connected to her in a special way and protected the treasured map.

"There's something new on the map," Hay Lin said. She turned on the lights in the dining room, illuminating the deserted round tables with purple tablecloths and wooden chairs.

"Good news, I hope," Taranee said, peering over her glasses as she walked into the large room. She looked ready to learn about new clues.

Hay Lin walked over to a table and carefully unrolled the map. Will, Irma, and Taranee leaned in and listened closely.

Irma could sense the mounting curiosity in the group. The map wasn't always a sign of good things to come.

"To start off, a new portal has opened," Hay Lin announced, pointing to an image near the upper right-hand corner of the map.

Irma was impatient. "That's nothing new," she said quickly.

"Let her finish," Will said, giving Irma a

look. Irma sat back and forced herself to focus . . . and to keep quiet.

Hay Lin held the map out, displaying it to her friends as she spoke. "You can also see that this portal is different from the other ones we've encountered," Hay Lin observed. "And, listening to the radio," she continued, "I discovered that its location matches the epicenter of the earthquake that happened last night!"

Will gasped. "Do you understand what this means?" she asked her friends.

It didn't take a brain surgeon to figure out the answer to that question.

"Trouble," Irma said. "That's what it means."

"If the portal and the earthquake are linked, there's no time to lose," Will said, with a sense of urgency. "Let's go and check it out."

Irma had to admit that, even though Will could be a reluctant leader, she knew when to take charge.

The girls left the restaurant quickly and rushed out onto the snowy sidewalk, with Will leading the way.

"I have a question," Taranee said. The serious tone of her voice made her sound like a TV correspondent covering a late-breaking news alert.

Irma couldn't resist. She held an invisible video camera up to Taranee's face in full news-reporter style. "Quick," she said. "Ask away!"

"Shouldn't we wait for Cornelia?" Taranee continued, ignoring Irma's one-girl show.

"I called her a bunch of times," Hay Lin explained, looking concerned. "But she wasn't home."

The girls continued to walk down the street.

Irma had a sneaking suspicion that *she* knew exactly where Cornelia was at that moment. And it wasn't her telepathic powers that were leading her to that conclusion. She knew her headstrong friend and what she was capable of doing when she was intent on something. But, still, it was hard to imagine Cornelia's venturing to Metamoor by herself.

"Tell me she didn't do it," Irma said out loud, making a horrified face. "Tell me!"

"What are you talking about?" Taranee asked, confused.

"Cornelia wanted to go to Meridian," Hay Lin explained. "To find Elyon."

"But she couldn't have done it alone, right?" Taranee said, her voice full of anxiety.

Her question lingered in the air as the girls dashed down the steps to Heatherfield's subway.

Irma didn't know what to expect, but that was part of being a Guardian. She had to be prepared for the unexpected – at all times.

ELEVEN

Cornelia slowly pulled back the curtain and peeked out at the streets below. "Looks like the soldiers are gone," she said.

She and Elyon were hiding out in a musty, wooden loft. After the explosion, they needed to take cover for a while. It was a pretty sparse setup – exposed beams, a wooden ladder, an A-frame roof, a simple bed, and a half-used candle. A chair was still knocked on its side from the earthquake, and several cracks webbed along the walls.

Elyon stood just a few feet behind Cornelia, her brown cloak blending into the beiges and browns of the room.

Even though her back was to her, Cornelia could feel Elyon's gaze. She knew that the time had come for them to talk. Since Elyon's mysterious disappearance from Heatherfield, they had not been alone.

"I was going through one of the worst moments of my life, and then you appeared," Elyon said tentatively, walking closer to Cornelia, overwhelmed by her friend's presence.

Cornelia looked at her old friend. For the first time in a long time, she felt that the old Elyon, her former best friend, was on her side. She had never imagined they would meet again in a situation like this.

"It's as if nothing had changed between us," Elyon said softly. She paused and looked at Cornelia. "As if everything was the way it should be."

"That's exactly why I'm here, Elyon," Cornelia explained. "Our destiny cannot be to fight each other. We were friends," she said, her eyes growing large. "True friends. Best friends."

"Don't say we *were*," Elyon pleaded. "We can be friends again!" She stretched her hands out towards Cornelia.

"I'd like that," Cornelia said warmly as she took hold of Elyon's hands. She held on tightly.

Our friendship is true, Cornelia thought. But thoughts of the recent past still crowded her mind. "But do you really think it's still possible?"

They stood there for a moment, holding hands, both remembering the close bond they had once shared. All the secrets and the laughter that had been a part of their history flooded back into Cornelia's heart, and she felt that at that moment they were as close as ever, that nothing could pry them apart – not even the turmoil of Meridian.

Finally, Elyon removed her hands from Cornelia's grasp and turned away.

"I know I've been wrong," Elyon said, balling up her fists in anger. "I did horrible things to all of you."

Cornelia took a step back. She was surprised to hear Elyon speak so openly about what had happened between Elyon and the other Guardians.

Elyon scrunched up her face in disgust. "Cedric changed my life. He filled my head with all types of monstrosities and lies." She paused and said, "And I believed him."

"And now?" Cornelia asked, her forehead

becoming furrowed in anticipation. She desperately wanted the old Elyon back. She hoped with all her heart that that was possible.

Elyon's head hung down. "I don't know," she said, now seeming even more lonely and uncertain than before. "I don't even know who I am anymore." Her eyes grew teary, and she turned her back to Cornelia.

Cornelia stepped forward and placed her hand on Elyon's shoulder. She wanted to comfort her friend, yet she was still confused by all of the emotions coursing through her. Everything she had known to be true was quickly changing. As much as she wanted to believe Elyon, Cornelia had a responsibility as well. She was a Guardian now. She listened carefully to Elyon.

"In Heatherfield, I had nothing," Elyon continued, looking rejected and sad. "And here, in Meridian, I'm the princess of a world that doesn't want me."

"We'll find a solution," Cornelia assured her, giving her a hug. Cornelia now knew beyond a doubt that she had to help her friend. After all, Cornelia had her fellow Guardians – Elyon had no one. Cornelia couldn't let her old friend down now. Elyon needed her more than ever. "I don't know how, but we'll find a way together," Cornelia vowed.

Just then, there was a noise on the roof outside. It sounded like footsteps. Cornelia grabbed Elyon, and together they stood waiting. Suddenly, a figure emerged, right through the wall!

Cornelia was surprised to see Caleb. A warm, white glow surrounded him as he stepped towards them.

Cornelia felt a jolt of excitement race through her entire body. Caleb came closer and got down on one knee. His long, brown coat spread out behind him like a cape; he looked earnest and sweet. Cornelia felt herself swoon when she saw his intense gaze.

"Meridian needs nothing but your light, Your Majesty," Caleb said to Elyon. He bowed his head, and his thick, dark brown hair fell over his eyes.

"What?" Elyon asked, perplexed. She stared at Caleb, who was bowing down in front of her.

Caleb lifted his head. His serious green eyes glistened. "The rebellion is ready to serve you,

Your Majesty," he added solemnly.

Cornelia looked from Caleb to Elyon and then back at Caleb. What was going on here? she wondered. What was Caleb talking about? And what was Elyon's *light*?

TWELVE

As Hay Lin led Will, Taranee, and Irma down the cracked, concrete stairs and into Heatherfield's subway station, she felt a bit uneasy. This feels like a large, old dungeon stuck in the middle of town, Hay Lin thought. The cool, winter crispness vanished behind them as they were greeted by a burst of thick, stale, subway air.

They crept cautiously along the dingy, grey platform. A rat scurried across the empty tracks and perched itself on a pipe.

This spot would probably never wind up on the tour of Heatherfield, Hay Lin joked to herself. If it weren't for her enchanted map, she would never have known that there was a portal located beneath the city. Come to think of it, she would never have imagined that she and her friends would have found themselves exploring the underground tunnels of the Heatherfield subway system. Many things had changed since they had become Guardians, Hay Lin mused.

As she forged ahead, Hay Lin thought how strange it was that it was freezing outside, but weirdly warm down where they were. She was tempted to slide her goggles down from the top of her head and over her eyes for protection. From what, she wasn't exactly sure. The general sliminess? The eerie unknown?

Having studied the map repeatedly, she expertly guided her friends through the dark tunnel. They walked along for what seemed like hours.

Plop-plop. Plop-plop. Water dripped from the overhead pipes, adding to the damp and nasty atmosphere.

At last, Hay Lin spotted a door with an orange light shining above the door frame. The location matched the one on the map perfectly. "There's a passage here," she called out. Then, sarcastically, she added, "I don't know about you, but there's no place I'd rather be."

"Yikes," screamed Irma, as a rat crawled

across her path. She did a little dance, moving away from the confused creature. Then she looked around in disgust at her surroundings. "The portals never seem to open at an amusement park," she whined.

Leave it to Irma to crack a joke at a time like this, Hay Lin thought.

Looking over at Will, Hay Lin could tell that her animal-loving instincts had taken over as she flashed the little underground critter a quick smile.

"Yeah," Will said encouragingly to the group, "but maybe we'll end up at the Royal Palace on the other side."

Hay Lin pried open the heavy door, and they all clambered through. "Well . . ." she said, feeling the atmosphere shift dramatically around them as they entered the portal to the world of Metamoor, "I think this is the farthest we've ever been."

Hay Lin's eyes grew wide as she took in the new surroundings. Nothing seemed familiar. She was pretty sure they had never been to this particular area in Metamoor before.

"What is this?" Irma asked. She gaped at the building in front of her.

A massive stone palace loomed before them. The building was flanked by several square towers with dozens of arched windows. The front half of the place was covered in red leaves and vines.

"Well, it's definitely not a building that we'd see in Heatherfield," Will said as she looked at the ancient structure.

"Maybe it's a nice gift from Metamoor," Taranee suggested, tossing one of her beaded braids over her shoulder.

Hay Lin took the site in, scanning the area for clues. Soon she spotted one. She ran towards a branch with bright red leaves that was protruding from the palace facade.

"Look!" Will hollered, pointing at the strange placement of the red-leaved branch. "This has got to be the work of Cornelia. . ." her voice trailed off.

The friends gathered around. They all understood that only Cornelia's earth powers could have created such a delicate, red-leaved branch. *And* one that grew out from a building, no less. Hay Lin and Will ran their hands over the beautiful bark, concentrating.

"She is in Metamoor," Hay Lin said,

amazed. "I don't know how she did it all alone, but she's here."

Hay Lin followed Will as she walked into the large palace. The foyer was enormous, with vaulted ceilings and dozens of marble columns.

If the place weren't so eerie and quiet, Hay Lin thought, it would be like the beautiful palaces in movies or fairy tales. The marble floor, ornate granite arches, and regally decorated colonnades made for an elaborate, romantic setting.

"Now the only thing missing is one of those nice little monsters that always tries to kill us," Irma said, gazing at the seemingly endless portico.

"Don't say that," Taranee said. "This place is scary enough!"

"Don't worry," Irma said with a wink. "I was just kidding."

But Hay Lin knew that Irma was only half kidding. In Metamoor, they always had to be on the lookout for the unexpected. As Hay Lin and her friends walked by a freaky-looking fountain sculpture – part lizard, part fish, part dinosaur – Hay Lin was glad to have her friends around her. How did Cornelia feel being there all by herself? she wondered.

Up on the walls along the gilded corridor were a series of ornate, gold-framed portraits. Each painting depicted a woman of royalty. The women in the portraits were wearing jewels and fancy cloaks and robes.

Hay Lin wasn't the only one to notice the strange paintings.

"Maybe you're scared because these faces are staring at us," Irma said, pointing at a picture of a pleasantly plump, bejeweled woman holding an iguana. Ever the goofball, Irma crossed her eyes and wiggled her fingers up at the painting.

"Who do you think they are?" Taranee asked softly, staring at the ladies in the paintings. She looked slightly worried as she studied the artwork on the walls.

"They all seem to be royal women," Will answered, gazing up at the paintings.

An artist herself, Hay Lin nodded in agreement. Yup, just a few queens, with no kings to be found anywhere, she noted.

"Maybe these ladies used to live in this palace," Irma suggested, trying to make sense of the art.

Taranee stopped and stared at a particularly elaborate painting. "Look at this one.

It's amazing," she said. She leaned in closer to examine the portrait. "Doesn't she look familiar?"

Hay Lin stepped forward with the others to look more closely at the painting.

It was a rendering of a young queen. She was lovely; with big, brown eyes; smooth, pale skin; and light-pink lips. Her face was framed by an extraordinary collar made of silky white and yellow feathers. A crown set with turquoise rested atop her thick, red, cropped hair, and two long braids stretched down to her waist. There was something familiar about this woman. . . .

"But, what . . ." Irma began.

Fshhh!

They all jumped back, and in an instant, the calm, serene palace changed. Water gushed all around them, rapidly flooding the floor. It was coming from down the hall – straight from that spooky, reptilian fountain, which was now wildly overflowing. Water was rushing and gurgling at them, faster and faster, surrounding them, rising up to their knees, and still coming with no sign of stopping.

Will, who loved to swim and spent practically half her life training at the sports center, was helpless. Even Irma, whose magic powers allowed her to command ocean waves, couldn't seem to control these weird, torrential waters that were swirling around the girls.

The force of the current was so strong it pinned Hay Lin's arms to her body. She was held prisoner by the water, and the more she struggled, the stronger the pressure became around her. "I can't free myself!" she yelled to her friends.

"Aaaghhh!" Taranee screamed, as a torrent encircled her waist.

Streams swirled up around each one of the girls, holding them in place like glue with the great force of the water.

The whirlpool-like outburst began to surge even faster.

"Will," Hay Lin heard Irma yell. "I think it's time you use the . . ."

"*Heart of Candracar!*" Will shouted, one step ahead of Irma. Will's strength stemmed from nature's absolute energy, a sort of total power that encompassed and amplified all the powers of the Guardians. When the powerful Heart was with them, the girls were united and strong, and transformed into their magical selves.

Hay Lin saw Will hold out her hand and saw the pink orb start to glow in her palm. The hot-pink rays of magical energy shot out in all directions, encircling, transforming, and strengthening each girl.

"Water!" cried Irma.

"Fire!" cried Taranee.

"Air!" cried Hay Lin, closing her eyes. She felt the familiar and intense power change her regular clothes to the purple-and-blue Guardian outfit, with wings fluttering on her back.

"Nooo!" Irma screamed, as the violent waves pulled her under. Hay Lin watched as her friend struggled against the dangerous waters while struggling to change into her Guardian form.

Whooosh! The water spun and flapped fiercely around all of them. The more they struggled, the more intense the current felt.

Whooossssssssh! . . . Irma's power fought to gain control over the raging rapids, but would it be enough to save them?

THIRTEEN

Elyon walked between Caleb and Cornelia through the chaotic streets of Meridian. The people of the city were distraught and confused after the recent explosion. For a long time they had suffered under Prince Phobos' rule, and now they feared that his anger would be greater than ever.

A crowd of rebels – green-and blue-skinned Meridian monsters, all sporting similar brown cloaks – swarmed around Elyon, Cornelia, and Caleb. Many were carrying their possessions in beige-coloured sacks slung over their shoulders. They were gathering near a passageway in the middle of the city – a gigantic, round crater that seemed to expand in all directions. Blue steam rose up around the group, past the city skyline, and into the night sky.

Among the crowd, Elyon spotted the family she had seen earlier, the one whose home had been burned down. The father pulled a wooden cart, with his wife and son in it and their few remaining belongings piled in the back.

"It's our last chance," Elyon heard the father say, as she gazed anxiously at them. "Maybe we'll find a better place on the other side." He turned away from his family and studied the gaping passageway in front of them. He continued following the crowd.

The little blue-faced boy stood up in alarm. "I don't want to go to that scary place," he said, tears welling up in his eyes. He looked so lost and frightened that Elyon's heart went out to him. His mother leaned over and patted his back gently.

Another rebel, this one extra burly, with pointy, sea-green ears, gazed down the passageway with apprehension. "Are we sure this is a good idea?" he tentatively asked the others around him.

Caleb stood tall, looking every inch the strong and brave leader. But there was a glint of concern in his eyes as he surveyed the scene. "If everyone passes through the opening at the same time," he explained, "the damage will be catastrophic."

Elyon saw a look of pain flash over Cornelia's face. "I caused this disaster," Cornelia cried out. "I should be the one to go back to Heatherfield and close the passageway before anything worse happens."

Elyon knew that her friend felt a huge amount of guilt after the burst of power that they had unleashed earlier.

"At least you *can* do something," Elyon said softly, lowering her head and letting her blonde, shaggy hair fall in her face. She felt powerless, and just as guilty as Cornelia.

Caleb turned to Elyon. "Believe me, Your Majesty," he replied. "You can do a lot for this world."

"I don't understand," Elyon replied, confusion spreading across her face. "You belong to the rebellion that is against my brother." She stared up at him, searching his face. "Why do you want to help me if you know who I am?"

"I think the more important question is," Caleb said, taking a deep breath, "do you know who you are?" He gave Elyon a compassionate but penetrating stare. "Are you ready to embrace your true people?" he asked.

Suddenly, the crowd of rebels parted, forming an aisle for the three of them to pass through.

"It's Caleb!" a woman cried happily. Her enthusiasm and delight quickly spread through the crowd.

"He's with the two girls who opened the passageway," observed a bald, green creature in the street.

"Will this passage really lead us to earth?" another asked skeptically, raising his scaly hand in the air.

Elyon watched as Caleb quickly and efficiently took command of the crowd and got their undivided attention. "Listen to me," Caleb said, calmly addressing the group. "I know all about your pain and great suffering. You have been subject to the cruelties of Phobos for too long."

The crowd stopped to listen. Ears, fangs, scales, and tails all came to a standstill, the gentle, trusting eyes of the listeners taking in everything that Caleb had to say.

"With deception," Caleb continued, "the tyrant took all the energies of Metamoor. And with deceit, he seized the throne."

Elyon leaned over to Cornelia. "What is he talking about?" she whispered into her ear. Elyon realised Caleb was telling them all something important, but she couldn't figure out what he was talking about.

"I don't know," Cornelia whispered back. "I wish I did."

Caleb continued addressing the crowd in a powerful and confident manner. "But all is not lost. The Light of Meridian is not dead," Caleb called out to the sea of faces.

"What does he mean – the light is not dead?" an asparagus-coloured creature asked. He shook his head. "It's not possible. The light is gone."

"The earth girl has made him crazy," shouted another, lifting a thick finger in the air and pointing accusingly at Cornelia.

"The legitimate heir to the throne of Meridian has returned!" Caleb announced in a louder voice, while keeping his cool. He placed his arm proudly around Elyon's shoulders and presented her to the group.

Elyon looked at Cornelia. Her friend's mouth had dropped open in shock and disbelief. She couldn't believe what she was hearing. And, from the look on Cornelia's face, neither could she.

"Welcome . . . Princess Elyon," Caleb declared.

Shocked, Elyon stood there like a statue, a warm, bright light shining around her.

"There is still hope for Meridian!" Caleb finished passionately.

The crowd stood still for a moment, allowing this new information to register. Doubt gave way to hope, and they all let out a thunderous cheer.

Before Elyon could respond, hundreds of Metamoorians were crowding around her adoringly. They smiled, laughed, and raised their fists in the air with glee. It was an overwhelming sight.

"We're on your side, Princess," said a sweet-faced, tubby guy.

"I held you in my arms when you were just a tiny baby," said a lively, wrinkled creature with long, grey hair. She reached out and touched Elyon's arm gently.

"You'll punish Prince Phobos because he's been bad, right?" said another, younger creature with electric-green spikes framing his head.

"Welcome to the city of Meridian, Your Majesty," Caleb said, smiling at her in admiration.

Elyon was overwhelmed and confused. "What do I do?" she asked Caleb. She didn't quite know what to make of what he had just said.

"Believe in yourself. . ." he answered calmly. "And you will find your answers."

Caleb's words were gentle and encouraging. Elyon felt herself relaxing. She closed her eyes and concentrated.

Whoosh!

Suddenly, Elyon found herself in a different place. She was in the middle of a calm, white, sparkly room lined with intricately decorated columns and archways. Before her stood five women. They were bedecked in ruffled, silk ball gowns, cherry- and teal-coloured velvet cloaks, long, brocaded robes, fur stoles, and jeweled crowns. One held an iguana in her arms.

"Who – who are you?" Elyon asked, breathlessly. She was so confused.

"You must not doubt," said a pretty woman standing in the front of the group and sporting long, red braids and a tiara with turquoise stones. She gazed at Elyon with big, round eyes and a kindhearted smile. "Find courage," she said.

Elyon realised that the women standing before her must have been members of royalty. That would, she thought, explain the jewels and clothes.

"Meridian has always been ruled by a queen," explained one of the queens. "Not a king."

"You must reclaim the throne that is rightfully yours," said another royal, adorned with a pearl-rimmed neckpiece.

The red-haired queen glided closer to Elyon. Her kind face was framed by an extraordinary collar made of silky white and yellow feathers. Elyon felt herself drawn to her and listened intently. There was something very familiar about the woman, which made Elyon feel calmer and more at ease than she had in a long time.

"Now, go and do what you must," the woman said sweetly. "Don't be afraid." Her melodious voice filled the large room. She reached out and gently stroked Elyon's cheek, smiling at her. "My daughter," she added, now speaking in a loving whisper.

My daughter? Elyon couldn't believe what she was hearing. This was her real mother? The former queen of Meridian, standing right in front of her? Elyon had sensed something about this woman, but now she knew the truth. Of course! She's my mother, Elyon thought. The resemblance was suddenly so obvious to her. They shared the same round eyes, the same heart-shaped face, and even the same long braids.

Elyon was overcome by emotion. She tried to hold back the tears, but they welled up anyway and slowly tumbled down her cheeks.

In an instant, the moment was over, and Elyon found herself back in the middle of all of the townspeople – in the middle of the chaos of Meridian.

The crowd was still gathered around her, reaching out to her, hoping she could help them.

"Don't go away!" a fern-coloured creature

begged.

"Please! We implore you. Help us!" another said, gazing at her with admiration and awe.

"You won't leave us, will you?" asked a shorter one, desperately grasping Elyon's hand in his.

"I promise," Elyon replied. She looked into their sad eyes and could not even imagine their pain. "But don't beg, please."

Suddenly, she heard deep voices and heavy boots behind her. Looking at Cornelia and Caleb, she saw in their faces that they feared more trouble.

"Give us the rebels!" voices shouted in unison.

Elyon turned to see Prince Phobos' henchmen lined up behind the rebel group – they had finally caught up to them.

The group of armour-clad soldiers stood lined up in a row, weapons poised. The burly men wore turquoise-coloured uniforms. They looked like a strange cross between ninja warriors and sumo wrestlers. In any event, they were tough, mean, and definitely ugly.

"Those who side with the rebels will suffer

the consequences," their leader threatened, resting his hands on his massive hips.

"I can make them understand," snarled another, raising his dagger menacingly.

"Bow down to your queen," Caleb commanded the thuggish soldiers.

Elyon stood mystified, wanting to help but not sure exactly what to do. How can I be queen when I don't know how to control this situation? she wondered.

A stocky, green-faced rebel made his way to the front. "Go away," he shouted to the guards, flexing his muscles and baring his fangs. His compatriots stood behind him, looking a little less confident than before.

Elyon saw a look of irritation flash across the leader's face. It seemed that the soldiers had finally had enough. "Seize them!" the leader shouted to his army. The soldiers raised their swords in unison and began to move forward.

Caleb pulled out his sword, ready to defend his fellow rebels against Phobos' wrath.

Elyon watched as Cornelia rushed up to him. "You can't do this alone," she cried, her face wrought with worry. Elyon knew how much Caleb meant to Cornelia. She understood her friend's fear at the thought of losing him.

Elyon held her breath as Caleb raised his sword high and took off in the other direction, his boots practically flying above the ground.

"Go and find shelter," he called out over his shoulder to Cornelia. And then, to his team of rebels, he shouted, "Run for your lives!" And Caleb was off to fight for the freedom of Meridian.

FOURTEEN

With a final thrust, Irma shot her hand up and grabbed the edge of the whirlpool.

"I'm not going to lie; the Heart of Candracar gave us a pretty uncomfortable trip this time," Irma gasped, lifting herself up and out of the bubbling water.

"I'm just glad we each got here in one piece," Taranee said, climbing up the blue stone wall that faced the pool. She wiped her glasses and gazed back down at the frantic froth beneath her. It rumbled with an unsettling *blub, blub, blub* sound.

Suddenly, a thunderous noise sounded above their heads. A few rocks came loose from the ledge and crashed down into the pool, barely missing the girls. Clearly, their entrance was interrupting something.

Taranee let out a gasp as she dodged a falling rock. "I take that back," she said. "Maybe I'm not so glad we got here!" Irma could tell by the tone of Taranee's voice that she was not so sure about the welcoming committee.

Irma poked her head over the side of the pool to see what was happening. She gasped in shock. Wow, she thought. This was not what I was expecting. A fierce battle was taking place on an elevated street directly above them. And they had definitely arrived in the center of the action.

Prince Phobos' soldiers were chasing after what appeared to be the Meridian rebels. There were swords, sabers, battle-axes, and daggers, all being waved in the air.

Irma surveyed the area. She spotted evil soldiers dueling and chasing rebels. And then there were the rebels, running, scared for their lives!

Irma watched as one chubby, blue rebel stumbled, falling down headfirst. She wanted to go help him, but she was distracted.

A loud boom and a tremendous blaze ensued. Irma smelled the smoke in the air and nearly gagged.

Quickly, Irma pulled herself together. It was time to get tough. She summoned her energy and flexed her muscles. As her wings flapped fiercely behind her, she suddenly thought of her dad, who worked as a police sergeant back in Heatherfield. He thought he was pretty tough. But he was nothing compared to Irma's current, bad-W.i.t.c.h. self. She wished he could see her now.

Irma watched as Will, who was the last to pull herself out of the pool and up onto the ground, tried to come up with a game plan. Hundreds of rebels were gathering around the other side of the swirling pool. Steam rose heavily, creating a strange mist. Will was surrounded by the rebels. "Save the princess!" shouted one.

Princess? Irma wondered. What is he talking about? Who does he mean?

For a moment, Irma was convinced everyone around her had gone crazy.

Just then, Hay Lin leaped gracefully above the rebel who had fallen. "Do you need help?" she asked, swooping him up with a gust of wind – *whoosh* – and placing a big sword in his palm.

"Whoa!" he replied, rather stunned.

"Unexpected, but appreciated!"

Hay Lin spotted Cornelia and flashed her a winning smile. Cornelia looked back at her friend and winked. Irma knew she would never have admitted it, but Cornelia was glad finally to have her friends with her again. The group was back together!

Irma gave Hay Lin a look. This called for some serious W.i.t.c.h. power. Together, they bent their knees, arched their backs, and held out their arms to join forces. A massive wave of energy thrust forward from their bodies. "An attack today," Irma shouted, "blows the enemy away!"

Whoosh! A gust of wind blew around a soldier, forcing him to the ground. He let out a yelp, revealing ugly, jagged teeth, as his sword flipped out of his hand.

"Your attack is almost as fierce as your rhyme, Irma," Hay Lin joked.

Irma couldn't help smiling. Even in the face of danger, Hay Lin was witty. Will, on the other hand, was the consummate leader. Irma saw her look around for Cornelia. Will saw her in a doorway, rubbing her hands together. It looked as though she were channeling some extra power. *Zzaap!* A bright, green glow encircled her body. Cornelia's long, blonde hair began blowing in all directions away from the miniblast.

"If you have a minute," Irma heard Will holler to Cornelia over the roaring battle sounds, "maybe you can explain a couple of things to us."

"It's going to seem unbelievable to you guys. . ." Cornelia started to shout back.

She was interrupted by a rebel who struck a soldier's sword with a frying pan. The sword broke in half. The gargantuan goon was horrified – and ran away, frightened. The rebel let out a cheer.

Cornelia continued: "But let's just say I wasn't wrong about Elyon." She had to shout to be heard over all the commotion.

Irma wondered what Cornelia was talking about. But then, she witnessed Elyon swooping up a young rebel boy in her arms and holding him close to her chest. He was thrilled to be rescued, and gazed up at Elyon worshipfully.

Irma saw Elyon huddle on the cement with the little green guy in her arms. "Shhh," she said. "It's okay. Just be careful!" To a rebel who seemed to be winning a fight nearby, she shouted, "Don't hurt yourself!"

What has happened to Elyon? Irma wondered, as she watched her protect and defend the innocent alongside the Guardians.

And who, Irma wondered, is that totally cute boy taking charge and battling the soldiers like a real pro?

FIFTEEN

Prince Phobos carefully surveyed the battle from his palace. He gazed down coolly at his soldiers being defeated below in the Meridian streets.

Lord Cedric bowed before him a second time. His reptilian appearance was slimier than ever.

"You failed again," Phobos told him, his voice booming with a brutal force. "You know your destiny, Lord Cedric." From his blue-and-white flowing robes, he sent forth several wicked beams of light. The light energy curled around Cedric's head and tail, forcing him into a ball.

"Noooo!" Cedric screamed, wrapping his green claw around his chest for protection against the powerful beams.

Phobos stood there stonily, rays of severe blue light continuing to emanate from his body. He glared at Cedric with great disdain. "I condemn you to . . ."

"Aaagh!" Cedric screamed out again in pain, interrupting the tyrant. His long hair flapped around him in the blue wind. "Wait, please, master!" he begged. "Give the people what they are asking for. It will make your sister feel stronger, and she'll be ready to be absorbed sooner."

Phobos paused and considered the suggestion Cedric had offered him. He needed his sister's powers in order to be focused and strong. By absorbing Elyon's powers when they were at their purest, he would become stronger still. Phobos craved this ultimate power, and nothing would stop him from gaining absolute control. He was now very close to the final stages of his plan to have absolute power.

"Fine," Phobos replied. His blue eyes were as emotionless and cold as marbles. "But don't fail me again, because the next failure will be fatal for you." He emitted an even stronger burst of blinding light. Time was running out, and his carefully made plans needed to be executed without any further delay.

Cedric's eyes filled with fear.

"Remember!" Phobos cackled angrily. And with great force he cried out, "Do *not* fail!"

SIXTEEN

Cornelia stood in the middle of a large crowd of Meridian rebels, with Elyon and Caleb at her side. The people of Meridian had fought hard against Phobos's soldiers, and their united and unfaltering spirit and teamwork had paid off. Now they were gathered in the streets to celebrate their victory.

Looking at all of the kind, hardworking, worn-out creatures, Cornelia's heart went out to each one of them. It had been a tough battle. She wasn't sure she felt like celebrating. She was exhausted.

And she was very worried about her friend, Elyon, who stood beside her, with her head lowered. She looked distracted. Cornelia gently reached out and rested her hand on

Elyon's shoulder. She hoped that her friend knew that she would stand by her – no matter what.

"We defeated them, for the first time," cried out a gleeful, bluish creature.

A pudgy, pointy-toothed guy shook his fist in the air. "And if we have to, we'll do it again," he grunted.

"The princess gave us the strength," beamed a middle-aged creature with scales lining her long neck. She stared over at Elyon optimistically. Cornelia sensed Elyon's growing tension. All of these beings thought that Elyon was their saviour.

"Hold on!" Elyon called out to the rebels uneasily. "I'm not sure if . . ."

At that moment, Cornelia knew that Elyon was feeling overwhelmed. Being a princess was new to her, and she obviously needed some time to get used to the royally big idea.

Nevertheless, there was a lot of excitement in the air. Cornelia was feeling very proud of Elyon and of her friends. She looked over and smiled at Hay Lin, Irma, Will, and Taranee. They had come to Meridian to help without even being asked. There was still a lot she needed to explain to her friends. She hoped that they would understand.

Hay Lin turned to Irma. "Looks like things are changing around here," she said.

"Um," Irma said, fidgeting. "I'm not totally convinced. Since when do things end this well – and this easily?"

Will gave her a sideways glance. "Don't forget that little battle we just went through," she said, sarcastically.

Cornelia wanted to fill everyone in on what had happened, but this was not the time. The crowd was parting and making room for someone to walk through. Someone whom Cornelia was not anxious to see.

"Where are you, Your Majesty?" a deep, familiar voice called out, sending a shiver down Cornelia's spine. It was Cedric – standing right in front of them.

Elyon stood still.

The crowd hushed.

What was he doing here? Cornelia wondered.

Cedric was dressed in full regalia – a long, turquoise robe, grey epaulets, and a heavily decorated, ceremonial vest. "We've been looking for you for hours," he said to Elyon. "Your brother is waiting for you at the palace."

Cedric approached Elyon purposefully, and bowed before her.

"Your coronation is near, Elyon," he continued. "And the prince wants to celebrate the occasion properly."

"Yes, I see," Elyon replied with sudden strength and determination. "Let's go," she said.

"Are you serious?" Cornelia asked.

Elyon turned to face her. She reached out and took Cornelia's hands in hers.

"Your destiny is to be a Guardian of the Veil," she explained softly. "This is mine." She said the words with fierce conviction. At that moment, Cornelia believed that her old friend really was a true leader and a royal princess. She knew Elyon was ready for all the responsibility that now lay ahead of her.

But Cornelia couldn't help being apprehensive. Cedric was not to be be trusted. "I don't trust . . ." Cornelia stopped herself and then started again. She had to be careful what she said. "You don't know what you're about to face."

"Everything will be all right," Elyon assured her. "I'll handle it."

Elyon gave Cornelia a big hug and held her tight.

"Cornelia, I will never forget our friendship," Elyon whispered, a twinge of sadness in her voice.

Cornelia hugged her friend in return and knew that their rocky past was now behind them. True friendship existed between them, and that was a bond that would give both of them strength in the battles to come.

When the girls pulled away from each other, Cornelia couldn't help noticing the way Elyon stood up tall and, like a princess, walked over to Cedric to stand by his side.

Then Cedric and his elite warriors escorted Elyon to the Royal Palace, where Phobos awaited them. As Cornelia watched Elyon leave, she caught sight of her fellow Guardians.

Taranee clenched her fists, attempting to be brave. "Well, I guess we can go back to Heatherfield," she said.

Irma put her hands on her hips. "I wish we didn't have to make another trip through that disgusting mush," she said, motioning to the large pool that had provided their entryway into Meridian.

"If you know of a more comfortable way, let us know," Will said, crossing her arms in front of her.

Cornelia listened to her friends, and she, too, felt uneasy – but not because of the pool. There was something she had to do before she left.

She turned and began to walk away from the rest of the group.

"Where are you going now?" Will asked Cornelia as the latter walked away.

"I'll be right back," Cornelia called back to her friends. Her mind was elsewhere. She was thinking about Caleb. Sweet, brave, wonderful Caleb.

I'll never see him again, she thought with a sigh. Except in my dreams. But I need to speak to him – if only I can find him in the crowded Meridian streets.

And when she looked up, he was walking right towards her, his coat and scarf blowing in the breeze. She felt tingly, jumpy, happy, and sad, all at the same time.

I must tell him, she thought. My feelings are too intense not to share.

Caleb now stood directly in front of her, a smile tugging at his lips.

"Um," Cornelia said, clearing her throat nervously. "I wanted . . ." The words wouldn't come out. She started again, this time mustering up all the courage she had. "Well . . . I wanted to tell you that . . . I've seen you before," she confessed.

"I know," he said, gazing deeply into her eyes and her soul. Then he gently touched her cheek.

Cornelia gasped.

Caleb ran his fingers through her long, blonde hair. "You don't need to explain," he said.

Cornelia's eyes grew wider. It was real, she thought with amazement. This deep, mystical, electric connection. It was true!

"It was written that Elyon would come back," Caleb explained. He held her hands close to his chest. "As it was written that we would meet again."

Does he feel, and has he always felt, the same way about me? Cornelia wondered. Could it be?

"You, too?" Cornelia whispered. "I've been

dreaming of you for so long." Tears welled up in her eyes as she recalled all of the times she had thought of him, wished for him, felt his presence without being able to see him.

Cornelia reached up and placed her hands on Caleb's strong shoulders.

"If we have loved each other in our dreams, the Veil will not be able to divide us," he reassured her, placing his hands gently around her waist.

"This feels like a dream!" she cried. More tears threatened to spill over and run down her face. She had to pull herself together.

Caleb looked sweetly down at her. He stroked her cheek just below the eye, catching a teardrop on his finger. Cornelia looked up at him.

"Do you know what this is?" he asked. The teardrop rested perfectly on the tip of his finger.

"A teardrop?" she offered, unsure of what he was getting at.

"Look closer," he whispered.

Suddenly, the teardrop grew bigger, spreading out and changing shape. Right before her eyes, it morphed into a gorgeous, white lily. It shone and sparkled like a diamond. Caleb held it out to Cornelia.

"It is a promise," he said.

Cornelia thought she was going to faint. She couldn't believe what was happening. She hugged Caleb tight, feeling his warm, comforting sweetness. What a special feeling!

"One day, we'll meet again." he assured her. He embraced her again, and she wanted to freeze that moment, that feeling of being safe and secure in Caleb's arms.

Behind her, Cornelia could hear her friends whispering. "And here I was thinking Cornelia was cold and rational," Taranee said with a chuckle.

"Looks like she is the exact opposite!" Hay Lin squealed. "Ah, looooove." She clasped her hands together underneath her chin, fluttered her eyelashes, and let out a long, exaggerated sigh.

"I bet someone's glad she came to Meridian to look for Elyon," Irma quipped.

Cornelia knew she couldn't expect her friends to understand all the intense feelings she had for Caleb. How could they, when even she was dumbfounded by his existence?

Cornelia squeezed Caleb's hand one last time and turned to go. She could feel his gaze on her back as she walked slowly away from him towards her friends. She felt many emotions – bliss, hope, sorrow, love.

As she brought the white lily up to her nose, she took a deep breath. It smelled more beautiful than anything she had ever smelled before.

Her friends managed to stifle their excited giggles as Cornelia came back towards them. She was a bit too tentative to look them in the eye. Still feeling woozy from her embrace with Caleb, she felt as if she'd just gotten off a roller coaster.

"Ahem," Cornelia coughed. "We can go now," she said, flashing a sheepish, sidelong look at her pals.

Her friends immediately surrounded her; at their inquisitive looks, Cornelia blushed even more.

"We can't leave without knowing a few things," Taranee said, her eyes brimming with curiosity.

"I think you should tell us more about what we just saw," Will said with a grin.

Cornelia knew her friends were curious and

wanted her to share what had happened, but she could hardly speak. How could she describe the way she was feeling when she couldn't even explain it to herself? She would tell them – later.

SEVENTEEN

Slowly, Elyon walked behind Cedric until they reached the Royal Palace. Before her were the tallest doors she had ever seen – blue, shiny sheets of gilded metal, reaching practically up to the sky. The palace was well guarded. Phobos certainly knew how to keep himself protected.

Elyon couldn't believe that she was finally going to meet her brother. A million questions raced through her mind. For a long time she had dreamed of having brothers and sisters, and all along she had had a brother. But he was evil and malicious. How could this be?

"Come in, Princess!" Cedric said, bowing to Elyon before the towering blue doors. His green tail snaked out from underneath his robes, curling at the tip.

The doors opened, and a bright, white light filled the room. Elyon blinked from the brightness, which now covered her entire face.

She opened her eyes, stood up straight, gathered courage, and moved inside. The room felt tranquil and mysterious.

She walked and walked down a long, bright passageway. Finally, she heard a voice. She looked up.

Phobos stood before her.

The first thing she noticed about him was his slate-blue eyes – they resembled hers but were more almond-shaped. He had a red goatee, and his forehead and chest were decorated with red jewels. And his blond braids – they were the male version of hers!

He was tall, with wide shoulders and sharp, chiseled features. Elyon couldn't help thinking he was an impressive sight in his long, flowing, blue-and-white robes and his crown with its turquoise triangle. Elyon noticed that it was similar to the one she had seen on her mother's head in the vision that she had had earlier.

"My beloved sister!" Phobos cried out affectionately, reaching out his hand.

"Phobos . . ." she said, breathless.

"I've been looking forward to this moment for a long time," he said. He took her hands in his as if he and she were long-lost friends.

"I wanted . . ." Elyon started.

"Do you know what pain is?" he asked softly. "It is not knowing your loved ones. I lost you when you were a baby. I took over a throne that was not mine. I would never have forgiven myself if I had not had the chance to give you back your throne."

He took Elyon's hands in his. "You are the rightful heir," he added.

Elyon took a moment to look at her brother and to assess the words he spoke. She thought about her mother and the courage that the royal women had given her. She stood tall and looked her brother in the eye. "Well, I'm back," she said. "Meridian will shine again!"

"And we'll be together," he said, pulling his sister close to him, giving her a tender hug. "Forever."

As Elyon hugged her long-lost brother, she wasn't quite sure what to make of his promise – or what to make of him. She closed her eyes and tried to recall the warmth and support she had felt when she was in her mother's presence. And then she thought of Cornelia. Her friend had risked so much by returning to Meridian to help her. The battle that the other Guardians had won had demanded courage and strength. She would need to have the same strength.

I must remember that I am the rightful heir and the true light of Meridian, she thought. I must be strong.

IT WAS WRITTEN THAT ELYON WOULD COME BACK, AS IT WAS WRITTEN THAT WE WOULD MEET AGAIN.

I BELIEVE THAT.

"I'VE BEEN DREAMING OF YOU EVER SINCE."

AND IF WE'VE LOVED EACH OTHER IN OUR DREAMS, THE VEIL WILL NOT BE ABLE TO DIVIDE US!

I CAN'T BELIEVE THIS IS REALLY HAPPENING!

DO YOU KNOW WHAT IS THIS?

A TEAR?

LOOK CLOSELY!

"IT'S A PROMISE."

"ONE DAY WE'LL MEET AGAIN."

AND HERE I WAS THINKING CORNELIA WAS COLD AND RATIONAL!

BUT SHE IS THE EXACT OPPOSITE. AH, LOOOOOVE!

SOMEONE'S GLAD SHE CAME TO MERIDIAN TO LOOK FOR ELYON.

UM . . . NOW WE CAN GO.

I DON'T THINK WE CAN GO WITHOUT SOME INFORMATION!

I THINK YOU SHOULD TELL US MORE ABOUT WHAT WE JUST SAW!

IT'S A PITY WE HAD TO LEAVE THAT PALACE IN METAMOOR! IT WASN'T SO BAD.

DID YOU WANT TO RENT IT FOR THE NEXT SCHOOL PARTY?

I'M GOING TO RUN INSIDE.

SEE YOU TOMORROW!

HEY! IT'S NOT WORTH THE EFFORT!

SHE CAN'T ESCAPE FROM US FOREVER!

SOONER OR LATER, SHE'LL HAVE TO TELL US EVERYTHING!

GOOD EVENING, EVERYONE!

YOU'RE LATE. I HAVEN'T EATEN YET, AND I'M HUNGRY.

DINNER WILL BE READY IN FIVE MINUTES!

UGH! SHE ALWAYS TREATS ME LIKE A LITTLE BOY!

BLING

WHEN SHE BROUGHT HOME THE **PUPPY**, SHE EVEN TOLD ME THAT I LOOK LIKE HER BABY BROTHER!

UM . . . WHICH PUPPY?

HER SAINT BERNARD PUPPY! MY GRANDFATHER CAN'T TAKE CARE OF IT IN THE SHOP, BECAUSE IT'S TOO BIG.

OH! I UNDERSTAND.

HE ISN'T THE PUPPY SHE WANTS TO EMBRACE!

CONTROL YOURSELF, OR HE'LL FIND OUT!

WELL . . . NEVER LOSE YOUR HEAD OVER SOMEONE OLDER THAN YOU!

YES! I KNOW!

MAY I WALK YOU HOME?

" IT WOULD BE A PLEASURE. . . ."

TO BE CONTINUED . . .